Five to Four

SUSPENSION
SPACE

James Krake

James Krake

1

Waking

My computer monitor was filled with pictures of corpses. No, I wasn't a teenager in the early 2000's who just discovered Mexican cartel videos. There had been an earthquake last month and an apartment building had come down. The press was still in a feeding frenzy after they learned the landlord had been cited for prior foundation damage. They weren't quite delinquent on fixing it, but they were a gubernatorial candidate and attacking them was great for ratings. The media had all sorts of dramatic photos from the dig site. Mostly the rubble. First responders were here and there. Every TV segment started with crying families and dirty kids. I had the real stuff sitting in front of me. The corpses lined like timber up and down the street. Most were intact, some weren't.

I had evidence package after evidence package after evidence package of the deaths; photographed by the city and signed by next of kin to identify and certify. An apartment building collapse was big money and someone had to sign the checks. That someone was me, sitting on the fourth floor of the Harold Miller Insurance Building two city blocks away from the collapse.

The entire department had groaned when we saw the smoke because we all knew it meant mandatory overtime. The rest of the world didn't stop dying just because of a disaster, and corporate wasn't about to take a PR hit for a politician's stupidity. Even if only a few of us would have to deal with the earthquake itself, work still had to be shifted around and equalized and some people magically called in sick and then there was Lucy.

"Bagels everyone!" Her cheerful smile drew more snarls than not as she paraded out of the director's office with a bag of stale bagels and the dregs of cream cheese tubs. People in suits and visitor badges filed out the other way, I could only guess who they were. Lucy certainly had no business being in that meeting except to look pretty and keep her mouth shut—the best form of brownnosing. Naturally, she hadn't been pulling her weight with the insurance claims processing. That had fallen squarely in my lap.

I was staring at my screen, completely zoned out and wondering if I had the mental energy to go to the gym after work, when I felt a cognitive dead zone approach me. It's hard to describe the void emanating from that man, the way his gaze can prickle your skin even though he truly, genuinely, does not care if you're slacking off. My boss had stopped behind me, chewing one of the bagels that Lucy had brought out. When I glanced over my shoulder and made eye contact with him, he swallowed. He asked, "Working hard?"

It was three in the afternoon and I still had a dozen

smashed-to-paste bodies to go over, but they'd be there tomorrow. I was ahead of schedule and finally didn't have to stay past four. "You know it," I said.

"You live outside the city, don't you Ryan? How's the traffic been?"

Traffic was all kinds of fucked at the moment because they were still detouring for the building collapse. The construction crews kept pushing the opening back because of aftershocks and because they were union jobs that paid by the hour to stand around. The candidate taking the blame was not the one their union supported, thus nobody could get on the expressway in a reasonable time. Rush hour refused to end, snagging me no matter how late I left. Between the gym, showering, and possibly an obligatory work beer, I normally never had to drive in it.

"It's been better," I said.

"Well, here's hoping that earthquake season is over. Don't need an overpass falling or something," Ed said, and ripped off another bite of bagel as he walked off.

I wondered if he thought they were something like hurricanes or tornadoes, that the weather somehow affected tectonic plates. The only thing that really could affect it would be changes to the magma and that was controlled by Earth's core. That might have some kind of cycle, something changing as time went by. Maybe a slip between relative rotations. It wouldn't line up with a year though. Nothing solar about it.

Lucy pulled me out of my musings with a surprise hello and a soft grab of my shoulder. Despite being Friday, she hadn't slacked in her outfit at all. It worked like a visual funnel from her hips to her lips. A high-waisted skirt to a short blouse, the low neckline was only saved by the light glinting off her gold necklace. That drew the eye up enough to be snared by the red of her lipstick, framed by her blonde bangs cupping her chin. She would have been ready for a modeling photoshoot if not for the cinnamon crumble bagel she was eating. It was the kind that had more sugar than a donut and oozed oil with every bite–my favorite.

"There another of those?" I asked.

She blushed and covered her mouth as she shook her head. "Sorry, I got the last one. They're good, aren't they? I got to buy them with the company card too. There's sesame bagels though."

I wasn't going to break my diet for a sesame seed bagel. "What's up?"

She smiled and put her hands together, leaning in as she said, "I just wanted to thank you for picking up the rest of the claims on the Pine Wheel building. I totally wouldn't have been able to get those done without your help. Director Xang says that getting them done will be super important for our end of year budget and all that, and we'll see it reflected in our bonus, okay?"

"Actually," I said and turned back to my computer. I tinkered around with the database, trying to pull up the full list again because I wasn't through it. "There's seventeen more that need to..."

She had left the moment I turned my back on her. I couldn't even see her head over the cubicle walls. I spun back around in my chair and snatched up my coffee mug. I didn't realize it was empty until I had the thing to my lips. The claims could definitely wait until after I had more coffee.

Normally, I had two cups of coffee, morning and lunch, along with an energy drink made from pre-workout powder.

This was because to get to the cubicle suite's free coffee station, I had to walk by Seamus' desk. He was fat and showered half as much as he should have, which left some kind of odor in the air like if he ever took his shirt off we'd find festering wounds. His nearly incomprehensible Welsh accent made it almost impossible to understand him and when you did understand him, you got gems like, "I bet that lawyer spent more time thinkin' 'bout sticking it in the blonde than about the case."

"What?"

"The lawyer meeting," he said with a wave toward the director's office. "Lucy was in there to give them a stiffy in the negotiations."

"Seamus this isn't highschool."

He laughed. "Nobody ever grows out of fucking high-school."

That haunted me the rest of the way to the coffee station, circling around in my head like a half-remembered song. I would have preferred the kind of ear worm where I could perfectly remember the beat but not one single lyric to search online for the name of the song, or if it existed at all. For better or worse, the coffee machine sputtered out empty and begged for water just as soon as I filled my cup.

Clock said quarter after three. It would have been too late to bother refilling, if not for all the overtime going around. I popped the keg off the top. Carrying it in one arm and my coffee in the other, I slid out the back door of the suite. We had a break area behind the elevators, which housed leftover chairs, an understocked vending machine, and a utility faucet next to the bathrooms.

The keg was only half-full when the door opened again and someone said, "Hey Drama. I thought that was you." Only one person in the entire building called me that, and only when we were alone. I didn't even have to look over to know it was Mikhaila Petrov, the other woman my age in the suite. In her case, literally my age—we had gone to school together. In the seven years since she shot me down, she had filled into her frame. I still remembered the awkward and gangly teen that waded through school gossip with her head down. Then she joined the volleyball team.

Mikhaila fished her wallet from the inside of her jacket, a much more sensible outfit than Lucy's, and slid her credit card into the vending machine to ring up a drink. Rather than looking like she wanted to be on the cover of a magazine, she was dressed like she wanted to walk straight from the office and to a bar.

I was wondering if she had a date as I responded, "Hey Mikhaila. I figured we needed some more coffee."

The can clattered to the bottom of the vending machine and I watched from the corner of my eye as she bent over to get it, then brushed back some of her dark hair to sip. "I don't care how busy we are, nobody is staying late on a Friday. How bad are you getting slammed by Pine Wheel?"

I sighed. "Only as bad as I make it. I work for Ed, after all."

She nodded and leaned against the wall as she looked at me. "You're not doing Lucy's work, are you?"

Instantly, I grimaced. "We're all pulling a bit of extra weight, aren't we?"

"Did Ed give it to you, or did she ask you?"

"Bit of both," I said with a shrug. "She came over after Xang scheduled her and Ed was there and it's not like she could do it."

Mikhaila took a moment to compose herself, pinching the bridge of her nose. "Have you ever thought about complaining? You could go to Renee."

I shook my head and turned off the tap. "It's just a bit of extra work. It's not going to kill me. Nothing to go to HR over," I said as I hoisted the keg up.

Her lips tightened into a frown. "Some of the department is going to get drinks tonight. It's Friday afterall. Meet us at the Ax Bar at five?"

The Ax Bar was the most yuppie bar in a five block radius of our office building. Drinks were served in mason jars, burgers came out in oil trays, and you could rent ax throwing boothes by the hour. I did like the food though. Meeting at five would mean a short workout, barely enough to break a sweat, but she had a point. It was Friday and she was inviting me. I'd be stupid to say no.

"I could probably do that."

"Good. Lucy planned it, so make sure she buys you drinks as a thank you," Mikhaila said as she headed down the hall and waved goodbye.

The last I saw of Mikhaila as she walked off was her in side profile, scowling from the moment she turned away from me. I kept wondering what she was upset about. Probably Lucy, some status squabble between the two of them I couldn't comprehend. Possibly a text message I hadn't noticed. Maybe Pine Wheel.

I kept thinking about what it could be as I trudged through two more claims. I should have been able to get three, maybe four in that amount of time but I was tired and the extra coffee hadn't kicked in yet. I wasn't too tired to think about what might happen at the Ax Bar though, and to hate the fact that I kept thinking Seamus was right. Maybe people don't ever grow out of high school.

I probably didn't.

Then, at five minutes to four, just before middle management could no longer stop us from leaving, the whole world fell apart.

2

3:55

I awoke on the floor, which normally only happened after heavy drinking. My head wasn't pounding, the room didn't spin, and I didn't have cottonmouth either, so I couldn't say I had a hangover. The only other explanation I had for why I would be laying on the dirty, coffee-stained floor of my cubicle suite–a hellscape of hair balls, candy wrappers, and asphalt grit–was that I had just suffered a stroke.

I didn't even get lightheaded when I sat up. No matter what I took stock of, I seemed to be completely healthy and intact. Not even a bruise. That was about the time when I realized that no one had come over to help me. Even if I had just fallen asleep, someone would have woken me up. It was the end of the day afterall. Pulling my phone out, I confirmed it was five minutes until four. There was no way I could have been asleep.

Not because the coffee would have kept me up, I was very accustomed to pounding an energy drink and accidentally falling asleep before the caffeine kicked in, but because the floor of the cubicle suite was raised off the ground. The six inches of cabling space made it echo like a drum when everyone started leaving the suite. It would have been like a cuckoo clock on my forehead.

But no one had come to get me because there was no one in the office. We had row after row of cubicles in the suite packed between the windows and the central hall. The architects had fit as many desks as they could into the building, and then forced in some more for good measure. I should have been able to smell three different armpits, especially Seamus', but there was no one in the office.

The place was dead quiet too, not even computer fans or the ambient buzz they used to muffle the din of phone calls. The air stood stagnant around me. The rudimentary noise cancellation wasn't the only thing missing either. Someone had stolen my chair and replaced it with a rigid, wooden chair. It at least didn't roll away from me as I pulled myself back to my feet and looked around. There was something hazy and indistinct about my desk, like I had someone's prescription glasses on. fRubbing my eyes changed nothing, then I realized it wasn't my vision but the contents themselves. Not only was my laptop missing–along with the monitor, docking station, and phone charger–but the paperwork was all fake. When I tried to actually read something there weren't any words on the page, just ink smudges like a low resolution video game. Just to be sure, I gave the sheet a wiggle and ripped off a corner. It was definitely paper, just faded the same way receipts faded after being forgotten in a wallet.

"What in the... Hello?" I had never ever heard my own

voice echo in the office, but it echoed back to me. I thought for sure the thumb-tack padding on the cubicle walls would have eaten an echo, but with literally nobody else in the suite there it was. Then I saw the outside windows. I tried to spin my chair to look. Wooden legs didn't spin.

Normally, the view out our window looked a bit like the world had ended. Half the view was consumed by the gravel roof over the auditorium, sky took the other half and left just a sliver of city between. Aside from right after sunrise–when light would blast in like a searing blade through the windows and blind everybody–it was a passable view for an office, mass casualty earthquakes notwithstanding.

Before me, an orange haze had replaced everything–blotted out the world and left nothing else. It looked maybe like a wildfire, but that at least had structure. A dangerous splattering of combustion as fire ate through everything, the glow of orange radiating through the dark smoke. This was just hazy orange, or maybe sepia was more accurate.

It looked like an old polaroid.

"Ryan, that you?" my boss asked.

I spun around. His bald head came bobbing down the aisle, black eyes peering over the edge of the cubicles. On the list of all people I would possibly want to see in an emergency I probably would have omitted Ed entirely. While he wasn't the kind of person to panic and make things worse, he also struck me as the kind of person that would just walk off to save himself and not even bother to tell anyone. "So I'm not alone. Where the fuck is everybody?"

He stopped in the same row as me and put his hands on

his hips. Jerking his chin at the window, he asked, "Do you know what's going on?"

"Chemical attack?" A decade of playing Call of Honor apparently had left a deep impression on my subconscious.

Ed cocked his head and frowned. "You think that's mustard gas or something?"

I glanced around our desolated office suite again. "Ed, I'm kind of more concerned about where the fuck everyone went. It's…" I pulled out my phone again. "Three fifty-five. The building doesn't empty that fucking fast, not even on a Friday."

"Your phone says three fifty-five too?" Ed asked.

I really hated talking with him sometimes. "What's the deal with the chairs? Where are the computers? Did I pass out and get carried to an abandoned floor or something? Did I get roofied?"

He shrugged. "That's a good question. I haven't seen these chairs in years, since before the merger. Whole place sorta looks like back then."

My heart felt like I had just chugged an extra energy drink and gone for a sprint. Keeping my words even became a struggle as I said, "Ed, are you saying we're in the past or something? Because that's stupid."

"Well we're in something. Did you just wake up?"

"I saw you like three minutes ago getting ready to go home. It's not even four."

He laughed. "Ryan, that was, like, half an hour ago."

Out came my phone again. I showed him the time. "Three fifty-five. Why are you trying to fuck with me?"

He still had that uncaring stare. "Ryan, it's been three fifty-five for the last half hour."

I checked my phone. It definitely should have ticked over to fifty-six by now. I wanted to tell him he was an idiot, but the clock did seem to be frozen. I didn't have a data signal, so maybe it couldn't ping for internet synchronization, but it should have been ticking forward regardless. Phone clocks worked just fine in airplane mode. Rather than retort, I set a one minute timer. Ed arched an eyebrow at me, but I ignored him and kept my eyes glued to the clock as the timer ticked down.

The alarm chimed and it still said 3:55.

"That's extraordinarily weird," I said.

"If you think that's weird, you should go look at the hall."

"What's in the hall?"

"It's not the hall."

"How is the hall not the hall?"

"Because it's literally not."

"What the hell is that supposed to mean?"

Ed waved at the door out to the stairs and said, "Just go look. You're not going to believe me if I say it. Go. Literally just look. Maybe it'll be different for you."

Of all the people from my office I could be stuck with, why did it have to be him? There were at least twenty guys with kids at home and I was sure they would be ready to break doors down and get out of here. Actually, Ed had kids he should have been worried about. He just didn't seem to care. Maybe I was the irrational one, but I marched over to the door and yanked it open.

There should have been a narrow hall with another cubicle

suite opposite me. Every single floor in the Harold Miller Insurance Building–both the insurance tower itself and the variety pack of start-ups leasing the other tower–looked just about the same. Suite, hall, suite, with conference rooms and bathrooms near the elevators. The only variations were for the executive suites near the top and the ground floor, where the cafeteria, auditorium, and so on were connected.

I was looking at the men's bathroom instead.

After a moment of staring, I reached through the door thinking that maybe it was a Looney Toons esque painting put up to mess with me. Not only did my hand not find anything, but I was able to step through and tap the tiling. The light didn't come on, but that was not the main concern at all.

I turned back to Ed and asked, "What the fuck?"

Ed turned up his hands and shrugged. "I told you it wasn't the hall."

"That's the fucking bathroom."

"Yeah, the toilets don't flush though. The water isn't working anymore. No electricity. Phones are dead."

I stared and let my brain process for a moment. I couldn't even hold onto a thought until my brain pointed out that while computers were all missing, the desk phones were still there. I bolted to the nearest cubicle and yanked the handset to my ear.

Not even a dial tone.

It smacked against the desk when I dropped it, but I just ran to the next one and the next one and the next one.

"Do you want to check a fourth? Or is three enough of a sample size for you?" Ed asked. He hadn't taken one step.

"Oh, shut the fuck up, Ed!" I stormed over to the other

hall door, still feeling the prickle of his stare on my back. I threw that door open too and once again was confronted by absurdity. I could see bathroom stalls and tile flooring. After a moment of adjusting to the darkness, I realized there were no urinals and slammed the door shut with a groan.

"None of the doors work, as far as we can tell," Ed said.

I turned on him. "What do you mean we? Who's we?"

"Mikhaila is here too. She is trying to find the way out right now."

"Then what are you doing here?"

He shrugged. "The same. I'm just going the other way," he said, pointing with his thumb at the utility closet at the far corner of the suite. My viewing angle was tight, but I could see it didn't connect to an overflowing pile of cleaning supplies like it should have.But, if that was the other way, then I pointed to the coffee station. "So she went that way?"

"Yeah, straight through."

Ed could take care of himself. He genuinely was one of the last people I wanted to be with in an emergency. Mikhaila ranked about as high on the list as I could put somebody, so I headed for her. First it was a walk, then I sped up. With the tiniest amount of mental encouragement, I broke into a run through my office and slammed my shoulder into the last door out of the suite. The door flew open and I staggered to a stop amid a neon glow like a thousand fireflies surrounded me. The colors were all different, like a rave club. As soon as my brain could piece together the shadows, I realized I wasn't behind the elevators–given the bathroom situation, that was no surprise–but rather I was in the server room. Hundreds of the specialized computers blinked and beeped, screaming into the darkness that they were on battery power.

All I knew about the room was that it was supposed to be locked to everyone but IT by badge access only, and that it was somewhere on the top floors of the building. That raised the question of just which bathrooms I had been looking at, but what mattered was the other doors. The server room, aside from being a jungle of cables strewn about the racks and floors in almost complete chaos, was a crossroads of sorts and I had a good guess which way Mikhaila had gone.

One of the other doors had been propped open by a trash can and I could see the phosphorescent glow of emergency light strips emanating from it. To avoid killing myself, I pulled my phone out and turned on the flashlight. While I could see by the light of the windows back in the suite, the rest of the building seemed to be in apocalypse mode. A dozen things could have killed the power to the office building–nuclear attack, political extremists shooting up transformers, climate legislation, or an earthquake–but nothing could re-arrange doors and rooms like a jigsaw puzzle. Standing in the dark wasn't going to explain anything though, so I chased after Mikhaila.

My phone had half charge still, so it would last just fine. I picked my way over zip-tied cables like hidden anacondas and crossed the server room to the propped door. It was the emergency staircase. Normally, it went all four flights down, but I only made it one story lower before I had to stop because any further would require swimming.

Water was up to the landing, still and quite clear. I considered putting my finger in it to check the temperature, but it could be acidic, or radioactive, or home to hungry piranhas. I only checked to see if any water had splashed out from, say, a woman stepping in and didn't see any such staining.

Why water had flooded the stairwell at least three stories deep I couldn't imagine. The fact of it refused to actually stick into my mind, I couldn't produce a thought from it. I had woken up in some kind of nightmare and that was all my brain could handle. Mikhaila hadn't gone into the water–why would she have–so I pressed on.

The only other door the stairs connected to should have connected to a small hall of unused meeting rooms that people would take personal calls in. Instead, it came to the side entrance of the cafeteria, which should have been on the first floor. Whether the stairs had been moved down or the cafeteria up, or if that question even made sense, I didn't know. There was light at least, so I clicked off my phone's flashlight and headed to the eating area. The cafeteria was just about the only selling point that our office building had, because it was genuinely nice. At least it usually was, depending on which local restaurant had the guest spot because the re-heated pizza slices the company sold were disgusting.

Looking from the top, the cafeteria was a bit like an arrowhead. Seating formed the point and body. Side halls to either tower made the edges of the broadhead, and the neck that tied onto the shaft was where the vendors were. The seating area was enormous and open, with at least a hundred tables arrayed beneath the glass dome. The sun and clouds rolled by overhead while the outward walls looked upon a grass park sometimes used for marketing photoshoots. The company had been scammed into buying these enormous metal sculptures that looked like Lovecraftian shoggoths to me, but there was at least greenery between us and the city.

All that was under normal circumstances. Now, clouds hung about the dome as thick and ominous as any thunderstorm, their orangish color aside. The haze swallowed the entire dome and made me feel like I was a colonist on Ganymede or something–whichever of the Jovian moons had an orange atmosphere. I couldn't see the city anymore.

Something I could see was a teenager standing next to the windows.

"Hey," I said.

She turned and I got a look at what she was wearing. What I had mistaken for a dress was actually an oversized hoodie that almost covered her skirt completely. The neck had been cut so wide that part of it slipped around her shoulder until she put her hands behind her head and grinned at me. "What?"

My mind blanked again, half of it trying to act like it was a regular day and some punk and snuck into the office and the other half was trying to problem solve a nonsense nightmare. "The hell are you doing here?" Nailed it.

"Looking at that," she said, pointing a thumb over her shoulder at the mist.

There was nothing out there that I could see. "The statues? How did you get in here?"

She snickered at me and put her hands on her hips. There was something familiar about her, I just couldn't place it. "Is that really what you should be asking right now? Didn't you come running in here looking for someone? These halls are, like, super echoey you know. Instead of asking me how I got in, shouldn't you be asking how you–or the girl–can get out?"

Something in my brain was screaming at me, but the warning may as well have been in a foreign language. Alarm bells but no meaning. I glanced around the empty cafeteria, finding only us and shadows but millions of years of evolution was telling me that there was something watching me. The unknown was about to murder me, but all I could do was set my sights on her again. "Who are you?"

The girl laughed and shrugged. "Relax. My name's Tanya and I woke up here just like you did. I'm not gunna hurt you or anything. I was just having some fun at your expense. Promise. In fact! How about I tell you that the girl you're looking for went out that door there." She pointed down the opposite side hall, the one that led to the other tower.

Tanya grinned at me, an ivory crescent beneath a button nose and sharp eyes. She was tall and gangly, with her hands stuffed in the pocket of her hoodie, toes turned inward. That finally connected the dots in my head. The voice was wrong, but she looked just like Mikhaila had back in high school. My brain had struggled to place her because Mikhaila had never looked so smug. Whether or not I had ever grown out of high school, I still had those memories.

"You might want to hurry though," Tanya said. "I think I heard her scream."

My head snapped back over to the hall. I could see the door at the end, hanging open and dark beyond. There was a hint of glow-in-the-dark paint, just like the stairs I had come from. I took one step to head that way, then spun back to the girl. "Hold on–"

She was gone.

"What the fuck!" My heart raced as I ran over to where she had been standing. I had only looked away for an instant and she was gone. The window pane next to her was missing too, and I didn't even know if it had been there in the first place. The mist stood like a wall, refusing to pour in as it pretended the window remained. In fact, it wasn't even very thick. The haze was nothing more than a thin fog that just didn't end. The modern art sculptures lurked in the pavilion like misshapen beasts and I could have sworn one was looking back at me.

The fear was stupid, impossible to be real.

I didn't have time to think through what had just happened though, not if something had happened to Mikhaila. I focused on what I could do and I ran down the hall Tanya had pointed at. There was another staircase but I was once again at the top. The steps led down, and weren't submerged either. I didn't even need to turn on my flashlight to see the body at the bottom.

I recognized the black skirt and matte-gold blouse instantly, even before I saw the blonde hair and pool of blood. Lucy was sprawled across the landing, not moving.

I swore and sprinted down the steps as I tried to turn my flashlight back on. The steps were all anti-slip, but that had limits. I could charge down in my boat shoes, but her heels had given her a split skull across the floor.

"Lucy, Lucy you there?" I asked as I got on my knees and cupped her head. Gently, I pried one eye open and stuffed the light into it. Her pupils reacted. She groaned and shifted away from me but couldn't focus her eyes. I figured that was to be expected after smashing her visual cortex, maybe. I wasn't a damn doctor.

Running my hand through her hair, it was immediately a sticky mat, half-scabbed together but still oozing blood. It was warm and I couldn't shake the idea that it felt like I was touching steak juice. I let my breath out and focused. The blood was still flowing, she needed pressure on the wound. That was the most important part about first aid. Pressure gave real medics time to show up and save them.

But I had no idea if real medics were even going to show up. What was outside? Nothing but mist. I didn't even have phone reception. Out of desperation, and with my other hand clamped to her head as best as I could, I tried the emergency dial. That, I was told, connected to every possible cell tower.

Nothing.

"What happened?" a man asked, looming in the doorway beside me. He didn't have a light with him, so he was backlit by window light from beyond him. I didn't recognize the voice either.

"She's bleeding. We need bandages."

"We'd have to find the clinic but... I don't know if you noticed this or not, all the doors are–"

"Yes, I fucking noticed that!" I roared at him. With a snarl, I stuffed my phone into my breast pocket to keep the light pointed out and took another look around the landing. Her purse was next to her, some makeup scattered around. Thankfully, it was a big purse not a little coin clutch or whatever women called them. Hopefully, she packed it like a mother. "Put pressure on her wound, would you?"

"Sure," the man said. "You got a rag or something?"

"That's what I'm looking for," I snapped at him as I up-ended the purse. About a thousand receipts fluttered away, so worn thin the ink had rubbed off. Her keys hit the ground, a heap of jangling metal. I only looked at the contents when he slid his hand over the ragged flap of oozing skin. He grabbed her by the forehead too, squating like he was afraid to get blood on his knees.

"Sorry, do you know her?"

I scanned over the contents. Wallet, receipts, tissue–I gave those to the guy and he gratefully padded his grip–phone charger, condoms, loose change, three different gym membership cards, and a packet of pads. It had been too much to hope for antiseptic and her hand sanitizer was completely empty. "For fuck's sake... Yes. Yeah, I work with her. She must have been running in the dark and fell. She's barely conscious. We need to get her to a doctor."

He scoffed at me. "Well trust me, there's nothing I'd like more than finding a doctor at this point. Finding a doctor means finding a way out of here. I've been stuck here for an hour."

I ripped open the pad, figuring it was the most sterile thing to put against the wound and had the guy swap it beneath his hand. Holding her head was hardly a solution though, I needed something to wrap around her skull to provide the pressure. A bandage, or rope, or tape or anything really. The only thing that came to mind was my own shirt. Rather than the whole thing–the blood would ruin it anyway–I ripped one of my sleeves off.

I had always kind of wanted to do that, but had never the justification to ruin a good shirt.

Lucy seemed to wake up slightly when I tied the fabric around her head, cinching the knot as hard as I could next to her temple. While the seam had shredded easily enough, I was afraid the tear would split the whole thing apart. She just squinted her eyes at me and asked, "Ryan?"

"Welcome back to the living–you, can you take her legs? We need to get her onto a table."

"What's going on?" she asked.

"You brained yourself. Keep talking," I said, slipping my hands into her armpits to grab hold of her. The other guy didn't seem overweight, but maybe a bit thick. In the dark I couldn't tell if he was muscular or not but Lucy weighed barely anything. I didn't think he would drop her. On a count of three, we both stood up and started carrying her up the steps. I had her bleeding wound against my gut. I could feel my own heart racing again, but I definitely couldn't feel hers. Getting her onto a table, in the light, and maybe getting her some water was the only thing I could think to do.

It was very disappointing when I realized how useless that was. Still, as we eased her onto one of the cafeteria tables I said, "We should get her water."

"Are you a nurse or something?"

"No, are you?"

"No."

"So, do you have a better idea?"

The man looked around and grunted at the smoky windows. "No."

I found myself spinning taps on kitchen sinks one after another and staring at them as they sputtered half a gasp of water and ran dry. The pipes were disconnected. A city losing water pressure was almost unheard of. Someone would have had to bomb the water main, or a hell of an earthquake, or we flat out weren't in the city anymore. For a moment, I just stood there, holding the rim of a sink big enough to butcher a turkey in.

If I was in a dream, it should have ended by now. I shouldn't have felt the tightness of anxiety in my chest, the raspy breathing of carrying someone up a flight of stairs, and it definitely couldn't have replicated the blood that was still stuck to my hand. Dreams were supposed to be fuzzy, illogical things; cognitive spasms and bursts of memory reinterpreted by a half-functioning brain. This world was consistently in-consistent.

I was digging through a room temperature fridge for drinks when I remembered the window. With an armful of water bottles and glass cola bottles–I couldn't tell if those had regressed like the computers or if the cafeteria was just doing a throwback–I sprinted back to where we had put Lucy. Her eyelids were still fluttering, her breathing shallow. The guy was supposed to be staying with her, but he was over at the window.

"Hey." I took Lucy's hand and eased her up, thinking it would help her drink. "You lost a lot of blood," I said, handing her a bottle of cola.

She nodded and tried to twist the cap off, still seeming drunk rather than awake. It wasn't a twist off though. I had to take it from her and use the edge of the table to pop it off. She still wrinkled her nose when she tasted the warm drink. "I'm feeling better," she mumbled, tucking her feet beneath herself on the table.

"Drink up. We'll get you to a doctor," I said, and headed over to the guy I didn't know.

"So, what do you think happened?" he asked, glancing back at Lucy before turning to the mist again.

"I think she tripped running down the steps in the dark and is lucky she didn't snap her neck."

"I meant about that," he said, sticking his hand where the window pane should have been–where the city should have been.

I frowned and leaned forward. While it was true the campus had a little park for photo shoots and a city tax break, that park was about ten feet below the cafeteria. It wasn't soft grass to land on either, but a ring of drainage gravel. Worse, this particular spot had broken glass glittering. Not the worst thing to climb down to, in shoes, but it would be a one way trip most likely.

At least, through the mist, I could still see all of that, until maybe twenty feet out where it just sort of vanished. There wasn't anything there, so I should have been able to hear traffic jams and wind howling between buildings. Sirens preferably. Instead, I heard nothing at all, as if the mist was consuming the noise.

Or that there was no city out there.

I said, "I don't know. I guess I don't read enough fiction to have a guess what the hell is going on."

"Nightmare?" he responded.

"Aliens?"

"Interstellar witches?"

"Copious amounts of hallucinogens?"

"World war three started with a chemical attack?"

"The simulation is finally breaking down?"

"Ragnarok?"

"Rapture?"

"Well you have more ideas than I do. The name's Chuck by the way. I work in Auto," he said, and put out his hand.

"Ryan," I said, and shook it. There was something comforting about the feeling of another human's hand squeezing mine back. It at least was real.

"So what do we do? Head out and hope for the best?"

Lucy almost fell off the table as she shouted, "No!"

I arched an eyebrow at her. "We'd help you down."

She looked pale, because of the blood loss obviously. "We need a car, don't we? We'd have to get into the parking garage, right? It's not like I can walk to a hospital."

I could probably carry her if we were still in the city. That would be ten blocks at the most, if the city could be reached by walking. I couldn't shake the feeling that we were in the middle of a very, very large spot of nothing, and I did trust a car to go straight more than my own two feet. "We can just circle around from the outside, right?"

"You have to badge in to do that," she said. "Do you even have your badge? Mine was missing."

Chuck smirked as I checked my pockets. He said, "Mine's gone too." My wallet was missing. I was even missing the emergency twenty bucks I had hidden inside my phone case.

"What the hell? Why would that be missing? Shit, we could just break the door... wait they got rid of the glass door didn't they?"

Chuck nodded. "We've got solid steel security gates ever

since the CEO got mugged. We'd need badges to open them up."

I pointed to the lights. "If there's even power. Hey, actually, Ed's here too. We should group up with him."

Chuck scowled. "Ed? Bald guy? Talking to him is like talking to a department store mannequin?"

"That's him."

"Lovely. Alright, well, why don't you stay here a moment with the patient and I'll get Ed? See if he's found anything. If nothing else, he's another pair of hands to help her."

There was a short discussion explaining what room connected to what, then Chuck headed off. I didn't tell him about Tanya. I wasn't entirely sure she had been real, and if she had been what to do about her. It lurked in my mind as I walked back over to Lucy and sat next to her.

"You okay?" she asked.

"I should be asking you that."

"Sorry... I just found it kind of... I didn't want to be imposing on you too much."

I turned my head and stared at her. "Too much, huh?"

"What's that supposed to mean?"

"Lucy, you impose on me all the time. You do realize that, right?"

She blushed and turned away. "Ah, well I mean sorry about that. You get kickbacks for that, you know? I'm not a demon."

"Lucy, you can barely sit upright. Now's not the time to worry about that."

"Nuh-uh, I can–" she slid off the table and stood up before twirling around to look at me, hands on hips. "Stand."

I picked up her empty bottle of cola and made a show of reading the label. "Doesn't look like this is alcoholic."

"Oh, I'm only a little light headed!"

I was about to lambast her for that, that she needed to take care of herself and get to a hospital, but before I could spit out the platitudes, I was cut off. It wasn't Chuck coming back to say anything, that would have been reasonable.

I heard Mikhaila screaming.

I was on my feet before I knew it. "Stay here!" I barked at her, and I hoped that she was stunned enough that she wouldn't go running. The scream had come from the main hall, a little spot of connection for the staircases to funnel into the cafeteria. The main doors were four sets of doubles, lined up between all the vendor booths, and where I would have gone first if I hadn't been told to go the other way by Tanya. It was the normal way out of the building, and Mikhaila's scream had echoed through it.

Some of the doors were ajar, barely fitting their frames and that had nothing to do with the weird nightmare. For a moment, I thought it looked like the doors and the frames were the wrong size for each other, then I flew through them shoulder first. The room had light, plenty of it thanks to the enormous skylight that now loomed like a sandstone dome overhead. I was in the welcoming lobby, a roughly circular space with the VIP elevators, the security desk, and a lower story to it for access to the parking garage. Sometimes, management used it for events, speeches and so on, because the room was enormous and had good enough acoustics. Clear across the lower level, I saw Mikhaila cowering against the security desk.

Of course, there was no security officer there. The phone was off the hook, dangling next to her, probably as dead as any phone back in the cubicles. She wasn't looking at it though, nor the doors that normally led out. She was staring down the elevators to the sub-floor. "Mikhaila! What's going on?" I shouted as I jogged the long way around to her.

She snapped her head up to look at me, then back to the sub-floor. She pointed but whatever sentence she tried to say came out as just noise.

I took my eyes off her and looked down the escalators. Blood covered part of the floor, a huge splatter of it. If I thought Lucy had left a lot of blood at the bottom of the steps, she had nothing on the grindhouse gore that was Seamus' crushed corpse. My stomach did a somersault, and that was saying something. I had seen plenty of horrible injuries, but this trumped them all. It looked like he had fallen off a skyscraper, or been run over by a steamroller.

The corpse my brain could handle, it was the thing that had caused it that I had to stare at to believe. It stood so still I thought it was a statue, some kind of animatronic prop perhaps. It looked like a lizard had been scaled up to the size of an elephant. It had pachyderm hide, feet like tree trunks, a tail as long as its torso and a neck to match. The maw on the front of it belonged to a dinosaur, except the teeth were human.

And then it twisted its head to look at me. I couldn't even see its eyes but I could feel it sizing me up and I could see the blood on its foot.

I felt my hand squeezing around Mikhaila's arm. We were both staring at it, like that would keep it at bay. The Jurassic Park lie that vision was based on movement flashed through my head right as the creature started walking towards us. The enormous belly swayed from side to side right until it planted a foot on the escalator. The mechanism grinded under the pressure. Something buckled from the weight and it looked away.

I hauled Mikhaila by the arm and took off running. The first thing my eyes saw was the door that led to the security office and I bolted for it. Mikhaila resisted for a moment, then came flying in behind me. Both of us nearly tumbled through the door and I barely grabbed the frame in time to stop us.

The room was tilted nearly forty-five degrees.

"Go, go, go," Mikhaila said, squeezing under my arm and clambering over a fallen table. She scampered hand and foot over fallen chairs and cubicles.

I took one look the other way and found the suite half flooded just like the emergency stairs, so going up was the only way. The escalator creaked and snapped again. I stopped thinking about it. Unfortunately, the carpet was so cram-packed from years of coffee spills and dirt that I couldn't get any traction on it. I had no idea how Mikhaila managed it, but both of us basically climbed the slope with our hands until we collapsed into a cubicle panting for breath.

As soon as I could, I sucked air into my chest and held it there. She did the same and in the silence, we could finally hear that it wasn't chasing after us. I didn't know if I would be able to hear its footsteps–elephants were apparently very dainty according to the internet–but I would definitely hear it smashing through the wall to get through the door frame. When my guts allowed, I climbed onto the cubicle desk to peer over the dividing wall.

We were maybe twenty feet from the door, thirty would be generous. The thing was not reaching through the door to come after us though.

"Fucking fuck," Mikhaila said, curling into a ball.

I shook my head. "Couldn't have said it better myself."

"That thing killed Seamus!"

Technically, it looked like it had stepped on him after he had fallen. Everyone seemed to be falling and getting themselves hurt lately. Then I realized what I had done. I swore and thumped my forehead against the cubicle wall. "Why did I come this way? Lucy and Chuck were back in the cafeteria."

"Ryan, what the fuck was that thing? I was just looking around and all the doors are wrong and there's no way out and then I heard glass breaking so I went to check it out and that thing! That thing killed Seamus!"

"It was like a cross between an elephant and a dinosaur. Like an alien or something."

"God damn it, it looked right at me. I could tell it was looking at me!"

"Do you think it's a carnivore?"

"Do you think that fucking matters?"

I slid back down the cubicle and shrugged. "Yeah, kind of."

"Ryan, the deadliest animal in Africa is a hippopotamus, which eats water plants. It kills people because it's territorial and what if we're in that thing's territory right now?"

"Calm down," I said, though I wasn't even sure that calming down was the smart thing to do. "We're in the office, not an alien's territory."

She grabbed her head and stared at me. "Our office is not at a fucking forty-five degree angle, Ryan!" She swung an arm to gesture at the suite, and bumped her hand against something plastic. It rattled and she picked it up with a sigh. She was holding a gumball dispenser filled with peanut M&Ms. "God damn it, we're at Renee's desk."

Renee Freeman was one of the few genuinely nice people in the building. Unfortunately, she was our HR contact and generally only had time to deal with employees getting caught smoking weed, smoking meth one time, and getting in fights with clients over the phone, geese in the parking lot, and management in the bathroom. She liked me because I didn't cause trouble and I liked her because she didn't make a habit of investigating me. The free candy at her desk was a plus too.

I took the dispenser from Mikhaila and shook it. There were only a few left inside, and one popped out. I ate it and found that it was dry and hard, but still identifiable.

Mikhaila almost buried her face between her knees and asked, "Why would you do that now of all times?"

"Checking something," I said, and didn't bother to comment about the missing computers and the worn out papers. "Hey... are you alright?"

She quietly leaned against me and closed her eyes. After a moment, she said, "I'm alright. I didn't get hurt anywhere. I just don't know where we are, or what that thing is."

I had to subtly untangle my throat so I could say, "Do you have your ID badge?" My mind had flooded with high school memories the moment her skin touched mine. Enough that it hurt and I had to smother them.

She checked her pockets and her hips, came up with nothing. "Shit, I must have dropped it somewhere. Why?"

"Chuck is back there. He's from auto apparently, but he's back with Lucy. That's also where my missing sleeve is."

"I was wondering about–"

"Bandage. He and I were going to circle around the building and get to the parking garage. I figure that even if all the doors are wrong, we can still go there directly, right? But we need a badge to get in."

"How's a badge going to help if there's no power? The internal doors all default to unlocked in a no-power state, but fire escapes like that only have to let you out, not let you in."

I slapped my hand to my face. "God damn it."

"Also, how do you know the gate would take you to the garage? Wouldn't it be just as likely to take you somewhere random?"

I frowned. "Well, so far I think that maybe the doors are still lined up with the right style of door, you know? The main doors out of the cafeteria were all double doors and they matched up with other double doors. The singleton doors are all over the place, but the gate to the parking garage is one of a kind, ain't it?"

"Aren't there like four gates to the garage?"

"Yeah, but they all go to the garage, don't they? And even if they don't, we can probably hop the turnstile for the cars or something. It's badging out that's the problem and you just said getting out is fire code."

"Then we don't need the badge. Let's go around and try at least. Worst case scenario we decide between walking through the fog or walking back, right?"

"I guess so."

"Then how were you going to get out?"

"This girl broke a window in the cafeteria."

Mikhaila froze. "The cafeteria? You mean the room on the other side from us as the monster? I'm not going back in there. Are you crazy?"

I sighed and slumped down. After a moment of staring at the drop ceiling, I said, "Let's at least take a look, yeah?" So, I led the way and quietly clambered back down to the door we had come in from. Looking at it up close gave me pause as I tried to wrap my head around how the door had been rotated in the wall. While the floor was at an angle, the door was seamlessly in the wall as if it had always been constructed that way; upright with the lobby. It wasn't something that could be rebuilt and painted over, there was no way to color match the faded crap our office was painted in. Maybe an artist could, but not a construction worker.

"What's the problem?" Mikhaila asked, perched on the edge of a cubicle wall like a gargoyle. She looked like a kid playing.

"I just don't understand what's going on. I can't escape the feeling that I'm in someone else's dream."

She tilted her head. "Not your own dream?"

"It's not dream-like enough to be my own dream. This is like a demon's dream or something. I don't know."

"You're not making much sense."

I grumbled and opened the door a crack. The silhouette of the monster wasn't waiting to eat me, in fact I couldn't see it at all. I couldn't hear it either, but that didn't mean it wasn't still in the bottom floor of the lobby. I couldn't hear anything and my phone was down to forty-five percent charge and still with no signal.

"Is it there?" she whispered.

"I don't see it."

"Well sneak out and look more."

"So now I'm the bait? I don't seem to remember volunteering."

"What are we going to do then?"

"Fuck this," I said and shut the door. "We'll find another way back, first I want to check something though." Going down through the tilted cubicle suite, I went all the way to the edge of the flood. I stuck my finger in and tasted it.

The water wasn't salty, so we weren't in the ocean. Not brackish nor swampy, just vaguely dirty. I spat the taste out and wiped my tongue off, because I was pretty certain the flavor was just the filthy carpet.

"So?" Mikhaila asked, half turned to the twisted door. I could conceive of a room collapsing into a lake or something, but not how a door frame could seamlessly rotate in the drywall. It felt like we were in a video game, like a dev was moving around scenery objects.

I said, "I don't know, it tastes like water. I hesitate to call it fresh, but it's not salty."

"Is it rising?" she asked.

"I don't think so."

"Put something to mark the water level, so we know if we come back here."

I frowned and looked back at her.

She shrugged like I was the strange one. "What? In case you haven't noticed, we still haven't found a way out of here. We're trapped with a man-eating monster. It could be hours more. That's enough time for tidal effects."

I stared back at her. The only thoughts that came to mind was how composed she looked given the situation and I wondered if I looked half as competent. "Fine," I mumbled and went crawling around, digging through drawers to find something useful. "Just keep an eye out for the monster, would you?"

"Why do I have to?"

"Because I would like to know if I need to run," I said as I picked up an old roll of tape. A few more drawers turned up a marker and a shaker bottle. The marker was labeled Sharpie, but looked ancient. It was the kind of relic that accumulated in desks after a few decades. There were a few people at our company like that. People who had worked at the same job, at the same desk, for so long you half expected moss to be growing on their backs. Thankfully, there wasn't decaying protein shake in the bottom, so I was able to tape the bottle to the window half-submerged without gagging on the stench. After marking the water level, I did my best to peer out through the window beneath the water level.

I expected to see more water, darkness, maybe a fish swimming by. Instead, I saw orange mist, which meant the water level inside the suite wasn't the water level outside the suite.

"We gotta climb to the top, don't we?" Mikhaila asked.

I glanced around the suite again, sized it up and realized that the other hall door was beneath the water. The only other way out was the back door near the coffee maker, just like our suite. We might have been in the HR office, but all the layouts were the same. With one foot on the lip of a desk, and my other trampling a Teamwork motivational poster, I shrugged. "Better exercise than going for a walk, right?"

She sighed and started climbing.

Before I followed her, I had just one little thought. I grabbed a piece of paper, crumpled it into a ball and chucked it as far across the water as I could. It bobbed and then started floating back towards me. "There's a current," I said.

"What? How?"

"Water must be coming in from the other door. That door must be under water and this is as high up as it gets before it leaks through the building. Remember that rain storm we had a couple months ago? When leaks were suddenly everywhere and windows were draining into the ventilation?"

"Okay, what can we do with that?"

"I have no idea."

So, I had no better idea than to climb up the cubicles behind Mikhaila and help her through the door. She was athletic, but she did not turn down a helping hand when she had to pull herself over the edge of the door. I came in after, trying to pretend I wasn't out of breath and ignoring I had just kicked over the coffee machine.

"Ryan, I think we're fucked," Mikhaila said, slowly walking away from me.

The air temperature felt like it had dropped a little, but then I realized it was the mist in the air sucking my heat. We were outside, one of the few spots in the whole building that had fresh air. Up on the seventh floor, the footprint of our tower drew back and left a balcony. The VIP rooms were above us, but here was a private enough spot for lunch.

Or, it had been before security shut it down to put up a

suicide net. Someone from our department had jumped off a few months ago after a few too many claims paid out to un-expected widows. HR had quickly implemented a policy that after only a few months working in life insurance, anyone who wanted a transfer out would get one. They were sup-posed to open the balcony back up after that, but never did

I used to eat up here all the time because it was high enough that I could tune out the sound of cars and city life. Once again, just like the window in the cafeteria, there was no city to drown out. Mikhaila and I stood at the railing and stared at an endless nothing. There wasn't even wind.

"We're not on Earth, are we?" she asked.

"Feels like a dream."

"A dream we're all collectively having?"

"Well, I think that's more reasonable than us being dead and this is the afterlife. How much would that suck if this was the afterlife?"

Someone else said, "This isn't the afterlife."

We both spun to face the newcomer, a young, blonde girl. She looked like she belonged to a track and field team in high school. A swing cut to her hair, athletic shorts and tank top, running shoes, and an unlabelled varsity jacket swallowing her up. It certainly wasn't the same girl who I met in the cafeteria. but she looked to be the same age as Tanya.

Mikhaila put her hands together and leaned down a bit to say, "Hi there, are you–"

I grabbed her by the shoulder and pulled her back. "Who the hell are you?"

The blonde snickered and shrugged. "You met my sister, didn't you? I'm Morgan, don't worry. I'm not going to do anything to you. Not gonna lie to you either. She's rude like that, not me." Morgan smiled and stood with cocked hips, one hand planted there like she had arrived to save the day. How a braces-laden kid could help, I could hardly imagine. On the other hand, we had more problems than the monster.

I asked, "How do you know we're not dead? That this isn't hell?"

Morgan snorted. "Forever at five minutes to four? Almost time to go home but not quite? Yeah, I can see how that would feel like hell to someone like you."

I pulled my phone out and checked the time. I hadn't even been thinking about that, but there it was. Four minutes to five and no signal. Forty-three percent charge too. That had to mean time was passing. "Where are we?"

Morgan shrugged. "First, don't you think I should address how I know you're not dead?" she asked, and continued when both of us nodded to her. "Haven't you ever heard the adage that you are a mind–some say soul–and you have a body? And what's death if not the destruction of the body? The big mystery is what happens to the mind after, but right now, don't you see that you have bodies?"

Mikhaila and I shrugged at each other. "Then where are we?" I asked.

Morgan paused and put a finger to her lips as she stared into the distance. "I don't know what you'd call it! But does it matter? You're trying to get back home, aren't you? Shouldn't you be begging for help?"

Mikhaila spoke before I could say something rude. "Are you able to tell us how to get out of here? There doesn't seem to be anywhere else."

Morgan spun around and struck a pose meant to be cute. "Oh, you'd be surprised. But come on, if you want my help please ask kindly. Say 'Please save us, Magical Girl Morgan!' and maybe I will!"

We both stared at her. Even Mikhaila wasn't quick to speak after that. I asked, deadpan, "Is this a game to you?"

She swung a hand dramatically to point her finger at me. "Yup! And don't worry, my magic is real, unlike that Hairy Pothead series that just made up latin!"

"The what?"

"Do I need a transformation sequence like Sailor Luna?" she responded.

"Is that supposed to be a joke?"

Mikhaila shoved me aside. "To the point, Please save us, Magical Girl Morgan. How the fuck do we leave?"

"Oh, it's totally easy, you just need to badge out." She stared and smiled at us. As the silence dragged on, she crossed her arms and kept her gaze on us. "No, really. That's it. Find the door out, swipe your badge, and leave. There's not even a rush. It's still five minutes to four. You can totally think of this as a little vacation."

"People don't die on vacations… or at least when they do, people don't stick around to enjoy it," I said.

She frowned and tilted her head quizzically. "Who died?"

"Seamus did."

"You sure about that?"

"Very."

She sighed and shrugged. "I mean, I guess technically you're not wrong, but really you should be worried about taking care of yourself. I'm here to be nice to you, you know?

I didn't have to show up and explain anything. I'm just trying to counteract my sister's mayhem a little. I'll even do one last favor for you. The way out is back that way," she said, and pointed her thumb over her shoulder.

Mikhaila and I glanced at one another. "Stay here and watch her," I said, and headed through the indicated door. On a normal day, the door she pointed to would have led to the emergency staircase. In a way, it still did. Rather than flights of steps going down however, I found myself at the very bottom. A far cry from the photogenic lobby, the door we employees used to get in from the parking garage led to a dingy corner of cinder blocks with elevators on one side and stairs on the other. An array of half-filled vending machines stood along one wall to distract people trying to cut out early. With the lights out, I could barely see the bags of chips and unwanted cookies.

The door to the parking garage was the first ray of sunshine I had seen in hours. Literal sunshine. It glowed like an azure gem, like blue hued mother of pearls. Light from a blue sky that I could see through a hazy distance beyond the glass door out. Not the orange haze that swamped this nightmare maze of a building we were trapped in, but regular sunshine.

I ripped on the door handle and achieved nothing more than a rattling of the lock. The badge scanner had a red LED on it, staring at me. I yanked some more. I tried kicking the glass out until my heel went numb. Slipping a credit card into the crack accomplished nothing with the deadbolt. Pulling the fire alarm in the hall didn't even set off a beeping; the lever did nothing at all. Finally, I picked up the chintzy plastic chair from the corner, hefted it over my head, and slammed it into the glass.

The only thing I broke was the metal frame of the chair–hadn't done that since college–and I nearly shredded my hand on the jagged spot welding. "What the hell?" I was pretty sure a pane of bulletproof glass would have at least cracked by that point. I wasn't so arrogant as to think I could kick in polycarbonate, but the door was just regular glass. I was in fact an expert in how much force it took to break a wind-shield–and the damage done to the body in turn–and I was well in excess.

All that effort and I accomplished nothing more than a sweat. I was unbuttoning my shirt when Mikhaila stuck her head in. "You okay in there, Drama?"

"I seem to be beating my head against a wall… wait, did you just take your–fuck!"

I darted past her, shoving my way back to the balcony only to find it empty: no Morgan. "Mikhaila, what the fuck?"

"What?" she shouted back at me.

"The girl!"

She recoiled and looked around the empty balcony, her mouth hanging open. "Okay, look, she was just there."

I groaned and squatted down. I buried my face in my hands and hugged my knees to my chest as I smothered my frustration. When I put my hands down, I stared at the gravel and tiles as I said, "Can we take a moment to recap?"

"Sure?"

"We are currently in a place that doesn't obey the rules of reality. My best guess is a nightmare, but the other plausible explanation is an alien simulation… of a nightmare. I guess also magic, but I can't think of anything we would be able to do if it were magic."

"Morgan literally said this was magic though. I get what you mean, but we probably have to assume this is magic," Mikhaila said as she walked around me and sat down at one of the lunch tables.

I joined her and stared out at the mist. No answers were out there. "Okay, so how about the girls? And the monster? They're probably on the same side, right? They don't look like they have a particular way to protect themselves from that giant thing, and they're not worried about it, so it probably doesn't attack them. What with them being witches or something."

"Seems plausible, but also rather super-sized for a witch's familiar, isn't it? Shouldn't a familiar be like a black cat? Or a fruit bat or something?"

"I don't know, I've played some japanese games where witches summoning giant monsters was pretty normal. Could be a demon sort of thing, right?"

"Demons aren't..." she trailed off as she caught herself about to say something silly. "Okay, if that is a demon, isn't that kind of lame to be one? It mostly just looks old and not in the scary, ancient evil sort of way. It's wrinkled from age."

I scoffed. "Maybe they cast a spell on it to keep themselves young by aging it."

Mikhaila rolled her eyes. "And what? If we kill the monster they'll suddenly die of old age and the spell will end? Are we really so desperate that we're using fairy tale logic?"

"Aren't we?"

"Maybe if badging out doesn't work. We should try that

first. Let's focus on getting back to our desks and see if we just dropped our badges back there, yeah?"

I nodded. "Alright, we keep looking for a way back to the others, find our badges, come back here, avoid getting eaten by the monster, avoid letting the magical girl wannabes cast new magic on us or whatever, and see if we can just leave like she said we could. I'm going to hope that the daylight through that door means that this place just isn't real. Whether it's a magical demi-plane or a computer simulation or Hell or whatever, I don't think driving a car away from it is going to get us anywhere."

She shrugged. "I kind of think that we'd end up swamped in water, like the bottom of HR."

"Alright, no time like the present," I said, and checked the third, and final, door on the balcony. It led to the middle of the central staircase of the building. Eight stories of doors. "Oh for fuck's sake."

"Do you want to try the elevator? If doors of a kind match up to one another, we might have more luck and at least, wouldn't require us hiking up and down steps."

"Sounds good to me," I said, and spun around to go back to the exit.

I hesitated next to the vending machine. The food selection was even worse than a Friday afternoon should have been, a week after the company forgot to restock. With no electricity, I couldn't pay for a snack even if I had my wallet. Technically, I would have been able to pay through my smartphone, and I supposed it was a shame that our doors still used RFID badges to unlock. Surely we could be at the point of scanning QR codes, but maybe running out of power would be too much of a hassle.

Hopefully my phone would last long enough for us to escape. I put it to airplane mode just in case. Didn't want it burning battery trying to roam or something.

I frowned as Mikhaila pressed the up button and got no response. Same for the down. "I guess I didn't think this through," she said.

"The no-power situation is really getting annoying. However," I said as I stepped up to the sliding doors for the elevator. I jammed my fingers into the crack and pried the doors open. The mechanism fought me, but grated open and beyond was the inner door for the elevator box. "Perfect," I said, and repeated the process. A moment later, we were able to step into the dark box. Mikhaila tried her luck with the floor buttons while I felt around to see if there was a utility hatch in the ceiling. Movies loved to use those, but I had heard on the internet that the hatches were all one-way locked to prevent people getting into the cables. It only took me a moment to find the seam, but before I could find a button, latch, or keyhole, the elevator shuddered and dropped an inch.

I blinked and stared at the roof.

Mikhaila took a step towards the door. "I think we should get–"

Before she could finish her sentence, I had to yank her back from the door as the elevator plummeted. The floor shot past us like a guillotine. She was screaming as I hugged her to my chest. I didn't have the spare thoughts to scream, more occupied with floating off the floor in free fall.

As sudden as it started, the emergency brakes kicked in

and hammered us to a screeching stop. We hit the floor and fell in a heap. Legs shot to either side and my ass felt like it dented the floor. The impact jarred all the way through my spine and rattled my teeth. The clang of metal rang in my ears for a dazed moment until I realized that Mikhaila was clawing my arms off of herself.

"We have to go, have to go now," she said.

I wasn't about to disagree, so I jumped back to my feet and helped her pry the door of the new floor open. She was through it before we had time to even look, and I didn't blame her. I only had half a guess myself what was holding it up, what had broken, and how long before it would crash even further. The only reason I had the guts to go through the door–a potential guillotine–was because I had never heard of an elevator actually falling all the way. Even in earthquake cities.

I had second thoughts about rushing through about as soon as my feet hit the floor. I blinked and realized we were standing in the atrium lobby; the very room we had been trying to avoid. Mikhaila stepped back, bumping into me but there was no way I was going back in the elevator. We had come out the doors meant for VIP access and as far as I was concerned, that was a dead end.

"Go, go, go," I said, pushing her towards the cafeteria. We both took off running and I stole a look over the balcony. The blood was still there, but the body wasn't. Neither was the monster. My imagination connected the dots and declared him eaten. The creature must have slunk off to the parking garage, or rather through the doors that should have led to the parking garage. They might have, if Mikhaila's theory of door matching was correct. There were only a few sets of double doors left in the building.

Before I could puzzle that out, we were back in the cafeteria. "Hello?" I called, throwing the door shut behind me. Mikhaila and I both jogged through the gloomy rows of kitchens and out to the light of the seating area. Nobody was there. The general trash from treating Lucy still cluttered the tables, but neither she nor Chuck could be seen.

"Where'd they go?" she asked.

I pointed back toward our suite. "Let's just focus on our badges. If we find them, we find them, yeah?"

"Hold up," she said, and went over to the broken window. She peered over the edge and out at the mist, scrunching up her eyes as she tried to spot anything.

My heart was still racing from the drop. I took the chance to sit down and collect myself. I was just at the point of confidence in my breathing when Mikhaila said, "There's something out there."

"Like what? Another building plucked out of downtown?"

She stood there until I rose and then she said, "I don't know, but it's something. If we do go out, I guess we should go that way. Let's hope for the badges though."

I nodded. "Tanya was looking that way too. Maybe there is something."

"Who?"

"The other girl, like Morgan… Shit, I should have mentioned. Was the strangest thing when I saw her, because she looked just like you did back in high school. I was confused as hell when I first saw her."

Mikhaila cocked an eyebrow at me. "Skinny me or regular me?"

I cleared my throat. "I mean, it's not like we talked much by the time you were… athletic."

She grimaced and looked away. "Right, sorry. We kind of… we weren't as close as we would have–as we were before, were we?"

How many times had there been a chance for us to talk again, after she rejected me? I couldn't even remember which of us had stopped it. Maybe both. "Come on, let's get back to the suite."

We headed back through the stairwell and hesitated in the server room. It seemed untouched since I had last seen it, but I checked the other doors out of curiosity. One was another bathroom and the other led to the main stairwell. "Not very useful," I mumbled, and we returned to our suite.

I didn't see Lucy, Ed, or Chuck, so Mikhaila and I went to our desks separately to start searching. The first thing I noticed was the carpet. It was sodden now. Every squelch made the dirt-matted plastic ooze water one step removed from mud. I could hear trickling too. A dispersed pitter patter of water that seemed to faintly come from everywhere. It was like someone had triggered the fire suppression system, but if that was anything like the sinks in the kitchen it would have sputtered out well before here.

The only explanation was that water was coming in from another doorway, from a room that was partially flooded. Depending on how the magic worked, it might be a perpetual motion device. If we were lucky, that would eat up the magic, maybe. Might kill the spell and free us. I doubted we would be so lucky.

Before something like the monster showed up, I put my head down and started digging around my desk. I turned over every piece of paper, opened every drawer, cabinet, and filing rack. I even pulled the bag out of my trash can to check the liner before stuffing all the searched-through trash into it. I tidied up pens and cables and systematically cleaned my desk so well our suite admin would have been proud. When that didn't turn up my badge, I got on my knees and crawled beneath the desk to start that search. I had to turn on my phone's flashlight, and ultimately for nothing. My spare pair of loafers weren't even beneath the desk anymore. All I got for my effort was wet knees.

"Find anything?" Mikhaila asked.

"No, you?"

"Nothing. What do we do now? Check HR? Think we lost them climbing around?"

I scowled at my desk and stood up. "No, let's find the others first. Maybe they've found theirs."

"Where are they, though?"

I shrugged and pointed to the only door that could be pouring water into the suite: the storage closet. Normally, it was kept locked with a key over at the admin's desk and had the prestige of storing the vacuum cleaner and a filing cabinet no one knew what was inside of. Now, it was open and, as we approached, dumping water into the suite. The incoming stream seemed to be pouring from the ventilation shaft in the ceiling, somewhere around the flow rate of a bad fire hydrant. Walking through the water flow was akin to treading across a beach, and I was amused to think that it was a good thing I had boat shoes on.

My amusement lasted until I found Ed.

The room beyond was the auto suite. I could tell because they had an enormous mural of a crashed car. Everything else about the cubicle suite was exactly the same as our own, down to the layout of the desks. The architects hadn't flexed their creativity much between the floors of the building. Even the printer was in the same spot, dead center of the suite and now Ed's seat.

He had his shirt unbuttoned, untucked, and speckled in blood. He had a swelling black eye and sweat glistening across his forehead. He was sitting on a desk, slumped down with fatigue, but he saw us at the same time we saw him. He took a swig out of a crumpled bottle of water and gestured at the floor in front of him. "We've got a bit of an identity problem," he said half-heartedly, nodding at the body laid out before him.

There was a second Ed face down on the bloody carpet, his skull caved in.

I stared at the corpse, letting my brain slowly analyze what it saw and come to its own conclusions. There were two Eds. One was dead, the other alive. I couldn't spot a difference between them, like one had crawled out of a mirror, through the looking glass or whatever. The only thing I was sure of was that this was a significantly bigger threat than magical girls or a mere monster.

"Thought I was hallucinating, then he stabbed me with a box cutter," Ed said, holding up his arm where he and Lucy had duct taped some rags on.

"Was that near my cubicle?" I asked.

"More or less. Happened right after that Chuck guy left to go look around," Ed said, waving vaguely in the other direction.

Lucy came running around the corner, arms full of vending machine food. Her eyes popped open at the sight of me and she dumped them onto a desk. "Ryan, you're safe!"

"Yeah, safe and sound Mikhaila–" I got the breath knocked out of me as she threw herself at me and hugged me. She buried her head against my chest for a moment, which I thought might be bad for the bandage, but she didn't seem to mind. I couldn't say I minded having her throwing herself at me, sorta, either.

"Oh my god. We thought you were dead."

"Not quite. Small doors seem to keep that thing at bay."

"That thing?" Ed asked. "What thing? The monster? Or?" He gestured at the corpse.

Lucy spun out of our embrace, and staggered, a bit woozy from the blood loss it seemed. "Chuck told you, didn't he?"

Ed rolled his eyes. "Look, I don't know who the fuck Chuck is. I've never met the man before. He comes in talking about lizard elephants and what am I supposed to believe? Right now damn near nothing makes sense. But that," he pointed at the doppelganger corpse, "is something I understand."

I said, "It was a four legged creature sort of like a dinosaur maybe? But with hide like an elephant. I've never seen anything like it. I think it ate Seamus."

"I'm sorry, it did what now?" Mikhaila asked, and Lucy seemed ready to puke.

Ed stared at me without blinking, without flinching. "If it ate, then it should be full, right? For at least a while?"

Mikhaila stepped in. "Excuse me? That's your reaction? Seamus is fucking dead, and what? You care about yourself only?"

Ed's gaze switched to her. "Primarily yes, and you'd be stupid to do otherwise."

"Have a snack," Lucy said, tossing Mikhaila a chocolate bar.

I wasn't hungry, so I refused with a wave. I didn't want to argue with Ed, not when there were better things to do. So, I knelt down beside the body and rolled it over. I'd never handled a corpse before. Closest was a leg of lamb I once failed to roast. The tension in that knee joint was sort of like what I felt in the rubbery corpse. I couldn't tell if that was rigor mortis already, or something else. "How long ago did this happen?"

Ed answered, "Fifteen, twenty minutes maybe. Hard to tell when all the clocks say five to."

I glanced at clock he was gesturing towards. It was stuck in the same position as every other clock. With no sun and no working clocks, it was getting hard to tell how much time had passed. Could have been an hour, could have been three. The corpse was still warm, and looked a hell of a lot like Ed. Somehow, seeing my boss dead on the floor didn't bother me as much as I thought it should have. Maybe a few years handling life insurance payouts had dulled my response.

Or maybe I just didn't like Ed very much.

The clothes on the corpse seemed old and out of fashion, but they were the same clothes that Ed had on. Timelessly boring. The face was hard to compare. Live Ed had one eye swollen shut, while Dead Ed had so much internal bruising from the skull busting that his skin looked like wine. His sclera did too. It wasn't until I noticed a bit of fuzz around the head that I found anything noticeable.

"Ed, do you shave? Your head that is."

"I stopped that years ago. Why?"

I wiped my hand off on the corpse's shirt and stood up. "Just trying to confirm you're the Ed I know and not the clone."

"Thanks for being so calm about it." He was calm too.

I shrugged. "Sorry, this just isn't actually the strangest thing to happen. It's starting to not really register with me, you know?"

"That's because you didn't see the fight," Ed said.

"Maybe." I finally spotted the weapon of choice. He had ripped the desk phone free and used that. The plastic was cracked and bloody, but he had put the phone back on the station afterwards, curly cable and all.

Mikhaila swallowed and threw her wrapper in a trash bin so she could ask, "What if there are more? If that one was Ed, does that mean there's going to be one for each of us?"

"Probably," Chuck said, walking down the hall to join us. He had untucked his shirt and he had an energy drink in one hand, a sword in the other. I had to do a double take to realize what he had was a griddle blade, the kind for dicing up stir fry and the like. He must have taken it from the fake Chinese restaurant in the food court. I had no idea how sharp it was.

"Hold on," Lucy said, and had to pause to swallow. "Are we going to have to start, like, using code words or something?

To know if we're all really who we say we are? And not murderous clones?"

Everyone took turns looking at one another. Ed broke the silence by saying, "Well, I'm obviously in the clear."

"Mikhaila and I can vouch for each other that we haven't tried to kill each other. So, yeah."

"And I've been with Ed," Lucy said. So all of our eyes turned to Chuck.

He froze. "Alright, now hold on, that's not fair."

"He's right," Mikhaila said. She had her arms crossed and shook her head. "The stupidest thing we could do right now is to start infighting. He seems coherent. We just need to focus on getting out of here."

"Did you find the exit?" Ed asked.

"Maybe," I said. "Couldn't get it open. I don't suppose any of you are hiding a sledge hammer somewhere?"

Chuck scoffed. "If I was, Lucy would be the one holding this." Now that he was closer, it did have an edge to it. A hairline of silver from handle to tip had been grinded onto it.

I shifted back and leaned against the desk next to Mikhaila. "Well, if we can't break the door down, then we have to unlock it. Neither of us can find our badges though."

I saw the confusion that caused in Ed and Lucy, who both checked for their own. It was Chuck who asked, "Are you sure it was the way out?"

"I mean, looked like daylight to me. Not..." I gestured at the windows and the smoke beyond.

Mikhaila leaned forward. "Does anybody have their badge to leave the building? Like, a fire escape would be nice, but so far the only door out is the one that needs your badge."

That cast a silence on the five of us, and I picked up one of the chocolate bars Lucy had gotten. Seemed like offbrand crap, but chocolate was still chocolate. I wanted something to chew on as I thought. Ended up chewing a hell of a lot more than I would have liked, because the nouget inside was staler than a civil war hardtack ration. It made for a good example of why not to eat while bored, or in my case; thinking. As I was trying to not break my teeth on it though, I noticed what was on Dead Ed's waist.

"He has one."

Everyone looked down. Mikhaila was the first to grab it, yanking it off the corpse's belt and breaking the retractable string. Sure enough, we had Ed's ID badge. A little plastic card, and possibly our ticket to freedom.

"Let me see that," Ed said, and snatched it away from her. She just blinked at him, too shocked to speak back. "Looks like mine. Got the fading and the UV damage and every-thing. But, you know what this means? It means someone or something intelligent has captured us. We've been abducted. Probably, every one of your badges have been taken so the... the whoever is in charge here could make copies of you. Like that."

Chuck scoffed and smirked as he asked, "Come on man, you think someone is in charge?"

"Isn't there?" Ed asked.

"Like who? This place is... I don't know, magic or some shit."

Ed twisted an eyebrow at me. "Okay, first of all, even if it is magic, there are wizards. Second of all, nothing hap-pens without a reason. This place is obviously the work of something intelligent. Random chance doesn't just rebuild a building room by room by connecting doors like this, right? And why are we even here?"

Lucy was the one to answer him. Maybe the blow to her head and loosened her tongue a bit. "Well, there was that earthquake, right?"

I frowned. I'd forgotten the earthquake. There had been one on the drive in that morning. Had there been one after?

Mikhaila walked over to the window. She looked at the smoke then over her shoulder at us. "Did we maybe fall through the world or something? What if this is, like, some kind of interdimensional sinkhole?"

Chuck laughed. "What? A sinkhole? You know those form from underground water flow creating a cavity, right? So, unless there was some kind of secret government base doing… I don't know, particle accelerator work? Beneath the city, how would we have undermined our own dimension?"

Ed shrugged. "Doesn't sound unreasonable to me."

"Or we're dead," Lucy said.

Again, I looked at the corpse of Ed's doppelganger. That was dead. As stiff as a corpse in a coffin. That was lights out, gone forever dead. We could still talk, act, live. I said, "We're not dead. Not yet, anyway."

"We've got a badge now, don't we? Let's just get the hell out of here," Mikhaila said, and marched past us to go back where we had come from. It made Ed clutch his badge a bit more tightly, but no one had a counterargument. What were we going to do? Speculate the problem to death?

"Here," Chuck said, and shoved a broom handle into my chest.

I took it before I realized what they had done to it, why he was bothering to give it to me. They had used some more of the duct tape to strap on a chef knife to the end as a makeshift spear. "What are we, cavemen?" I asked.

Chuck snorted. "You want to fight a monster unarmed? Besides, if I give you this, I will know that you are you. It's like a totem. The missing sleeve helps too."

I jerked my head towards the others. "And them?"

"Not enough to go around. I'd give it to Ed there, but he's injured now. Besides, you're young and strong. You'll fight, right?"

I took a breath and nodded. "As long as the goal is to not fight."

Mikhaila rolled her eyes. "How about we just get out of here?"

"Should somebody scout?" Lucy asked.

"No splitting up," Ed ordered, and took the lead. He had a slight limp–must have been bruised somewhere. Our little troupe of office workers got in line and headed to the exit.

We made it as far as the cafeteria before we were stopped by Tanya. Mikhaila's jaw dropped–I figured I hadn't quite prepared her for the shock.Standing atop one of the cafeteria tables, she grinned down at us. It was a bully's smile.

"Are you sure this is right to do? When you've got a Judas among you?"

Mikhaila stepped forward, her eyebrows furrowed as she demanded, "Who the hell are you?"

The teenager snickered. "I'm Tanya. You must be wondering why I look like you."

I side-eye'd Ed, who hadn't said anything yet. He must not

have known what to make of the situation either and we all just listened to Mikhaila respond. "Yeah, I am."

"Too bad," Tanya said, and stuck her tongue out at her. "And you... Chuck. Long time no see."

"Fuck off," Chuck responded, not missing a beat.

Mikhaila said, "Are you with that other girl? The blonde? Morgan. She said she was a witch."

"Am I really the one you need to be concerned about?"

I stepped up. "The one about to be in danger here, is you, you little twerp. Who are you? What is this place?"

Tanya laughed. "If you really must know, I'm an artificial construct sent here by an advanced alien species to perform morality experiments on you bipedal apes. This is a virtual reality created in the fourth dimension as a laboratory."

Ed broke the ensuing silence. "If that's the case, where are the unstoppable trolleys? Why aren't we getting offered bribes to betray one another?"

Tanya shrugged. "You're the control group."

"How do we leave?" I asked. "If this is an experiment, which I have my doubts about. You're too smug. I'd like to revoke whatever consent you think I gave you. If you're so high and mighty to be ethically testing us then let us go. Seamus already died!"

"Did he?" she asked, and somehow managed to look even more smug. "If you want to leave, you already know how. Just badge out and go."

"So who's the Judas? Who's betraying us?" Mikhaila asked.

"She's bullshitting," I said. "I don't know what precisely, but she's obviously lying about something."

"Sorry to say, but that's wrong," Tanya said. "But I do think I'm starting to dislike you, Ryan."

"I say we just leave," Chuck said. "We know where the door is, we have a badge to open it up. Let's just get out of here before that monster shows up."

"How rude," Tanya said, dramatically pouting and planting her fists on her hips. "Builder is no monster! Well, I guess it depends on your definitions. Oh, Builder!"

My mouth went dry and I grabbed Mikhaila by the elbow. "We've gotta go," I said and tried to drag her away.

"No, hold on, somebody help me grab this so-called alien," Lucy said, taking a step closer to Tanya.

Ed seemed to be in agreement with her, maybe he was planning to drag her out of the building with us. That distracted him from hearing the glass breaking overhead. The atrium dome of glass above the cafeteria was not designed to be load bearing. It barely kept the rain out. When the four legged monster, Builder, stepped onto it, the framework crumpled like the steel was nothing more than plastic. Sheets of glass shattered, others fell in solid panes that exploded across tables.

I hauled Mikhaila away as the monster dropped down after. The floor shook beneath us when it landed, knocking her off her feet. "Come on, come on!"

Then Lucy screamed for help.

She had tripped. I could see blood on the ground. She was hyperventilating as the man-eating thing sniffed the air and sought her out. I could see the wide-eyed panic in her face and Ed was nowhere to be seen.

"You stupid idiot, run!" Mikhaila screamed, but Lucy didn't even budge.

"For fuck's sake! You, go!" I ordered, shoving Mikhaila to the doors out. I wanted her, at least, to get out–with Ed and the badge preferably. Maybe they could get help. For now, I had a stupid makeshift spear for a reason.

Chuck hadn't fled. He was circling around the thing with the cooking blade in his hand. I saw him lick his lips and glance over as I returned. "How the hell do we fight this thing anyways?"

That got the monster's attention. The big head swung over and it growled at him. While Chuck yelped and backed away, I grabbed Lucy by her shirt. She was light, or maybe I was high on adrenaline, either way I threw her back to her feet and kept the tip of my makeshift spear pointed at the thing called Builder.

Up close, it felt like I was facing off against the mutant child of an elephant and a brontosaur. The mouth was wider than my shoulders and its back towered over my head. My hands started to shake as I pointed the bit of kitchen steel at the thing and I kept seeing Seamus' corpse in my head again and again.

I should have done something, at least run away.

Chuck did something. That made him more of a man than me, or maybe just stupider. He stepped in and swung hard. The cooking blade hacked into the monster's flank. It chopped in and stuck fast. The hide seemed to grip the steel without even bleeding. Muscles like hydraulic pistons clenched up and bulged as the monster reared away.

Chuck pulled his weapon free, barely, but his face had gone pale.

For an instant, I stood transfixed. I could hear glass crunching beneath Chuck's shoes and the monster breathing. And I heard Tanya chide us, "How cruel. What did Builder ever do to you? I know! Get rid of them, would you please?"

Any doubt in my mind that the girls were involved vanished. Alien constructs still didn't sit right with me, but the monster obeyed her. Stupidly, both me and Chuck took our attention off the monster and tried to spot the girl.

Builder swung its hips and cleaved its thick tail through the tables and chairs. It swept them up like trash and threw them into Chuck. I saw him throw up his arms and heard him scream, but then he was gone.

Then I was screaming. Pure instinct, I stabbed forward and stuffed the knife into the monster's throat. It felt like I had stabbed into a tree trunk, but it went in.

The monster quailed and twisted, ripping the spear from my grasp as it turned to look at me. With a shake of its head, the cable ties snapped off and left the knife in its throat, me weaponless, and it very pissed off.

Lucy finally said something useful, and shouted, "Run!"

I couldn't imagine a single thing wrong with her suggestion. The two of us turned our backs and ran, abandoning Chuck. Builder charged after us, stomping through the cafeteria and knocking away tables and chairs like a rampaging bull. They barely slowed it down, but barely was all we needed.

Back out of the cafeteria, we returned to the server room. I nearly tripped over the cables, and in the moment of dark confusion while I tried to turn to the door back to our suite, Builder's head rammed through the door behind us.

Lucy grabbed me by my shirt and yanked. Incisors the size of shovels gnashed shut just above me. They were human teeth. Peeled open and trying to bite my head off, I saw the mouth inside was a human's but stretched to a gigantic size.

I hit the ground in a heap with Lucy, cables jamming into my back so hard I couldn't breathe. Both of us scrambled, kicking and crawling and grabbing anything and everything. We knocked server racks over as the monster thrashed and its shoulders cracked the wall between us and it. Behind us was a door and we went through that too.

From the feel of it, the wall was cinder block. Not the drywall partitions of the middle of a skyscraper, but foundational cinder block. "Go, go, go," I urged and we dove into the dark confines of an unknown room. Behind us, the monster ripped through the wall and stamped through the computers. I could hear snapping plastic and breaking metal as it forced itself in. Then the head snaked through the second door and again teeth snapped at us.

But that wall held.

Concrete and brick held it at bay, and left the two of us in complete darkness. We were stuck in a bathroom, with no lights. Worse, water was trickling in through the roof ventilation shaft. I tried to ignore it, which was easy enough to do while I thought Builder would smash the wall down and eat us. Then seconds turned to minutes and the damn monster laid down in the server room. That was when the trickling drip and spatter of water against tile started to grate my nerves.

It sounded like a leaky shower. The noise dug through my skull until I almost felt nauseous. Waterfalls were supposed to be peaceful, but there was just something wrong about this. Maybe it was the lack of wind, no leaves to rustle. Or it was how utterly sterile everything was; no flowers and no detritus. There were no insects buzzing nor birds chirping. It was just the water.

I stood up.

"What are you doing?" Lucy asked.

I had to grope around in the darkness, feeling my way from wall to stall and over to the water. The puddle sloshed against my shoes, but at least the boat shoes were good for something. I wasn't going to slip. "Gunna try to do something about this."

"It's falling out of the ceiling. What are you–"

I grabbed the edge of the vent, dug my fingers through the drop ceiling tile, and tore the cover off. It was only held on by the shittiest of m4 bolts, no longer than a pencil eraser. Water dumped across my face, which would have been refreshing if I liked cold showers.

Lucy stood up as the sudden flood of water washed over to her, then receded back to the floor drain. "I always forget just how tall you are, Ryan."

"That's because I'm always sitting."

"How tall are you, exactly?"

"Six one." The ventilation shaft was completely black, but the dump of water had just been because of the panel I had torn off. The flow had already gone back to a trickle. Unfortunately, we were in a corporate bathroom, which meant there were no towels. I improvised with my shirt.

"Here, I think my phone still has some charge," Lucy said, lighting up the screen of her smartphone. Then her flashlight lit up the bathroom.

I could finally see what I was doing, so I delicately wadded my shirt up and stuffed it into the shaft like a little dam. Thankfully, it held the water back and I didn't have to keep listening to it.

Which, of course, meant I had to listen to the monster breathing outside.

"You know, you look good in a t-shirt. How much do you work out?" Lucy asked, eyeing me up like we were in a nightclub.

I grimaced. Lucy was a prime example of why I wore baggy clothes. "Regularly," I said, and took a seat on the sink counter. I slouched and put my hands together, but she still stared at me.

"You need to buy yourself some tailored shirts or something. You dress like a corporate ogre… you sell yourself way too short."

I grimaced. "Lucy, did you forget there's a man-eating monster waiting for us to step around that corner?"

She planted a hand on her hip. "I'm damn well trying to. You expect me to just sit here and stew? No thank you. As long as it can't get in here I would oh so very much prefer to think about anything else. Okay?"

"Look, Mikhaila, Ed, Chuck, they're going to get out and get us help. They know we're still in here. They won't just abandon us."

"Okay, sure, but until then, talk. Please."

I shook my head. "Turn the light off. We can't recharge it

and we might need it later." After she powered her phone off, she sat next to me and I said, "I think you might be the only person in our entire office that actually thinks about fashion."

"Plenty of women do, you just don't notice."

I cocked an eyebrow at her. "Most of our coworkers are in their late forties and look worse than drug addicts."

"That's because a lot of them probably are drug addicts."

"Point, but that doesn't change anything. Have you ever spoken to Renee in HR? She has some stories about the absolute lack of human decency in this building that will make you run for the hills. We're lucky that most of them have been fired and replaced. Normal people don't stick around an insurance company for long. You definitely are the odd one out."

"Because I coordinate my outfits? Or because I'm normal?" I laughed.

"Because I'm not normal. Or like, I mean I probably am normal but in the nihilistic sense that what we think is normal doesn't really exist. It's a fake standard no one really lives up to, you know? I'm not making sense am I?"

"You're making enough sense," I said, and I simply thought that she wouldn't be winning any speaking awards for her ability to phrase things.

When she realized the silence between us was stretching, she reached back for something else to fill the space. She didn't explain why she wasn't normal, but she asked, "So how long have you been working out for?"

"About six years now. I started right before college."

"Oh? You're one of those guys that went and got buff to pick up chicks in college?"

"No, I don't really pick up girls. You've seen me at night-clubs, haven't you? I can chat with people I know, but you ask me to introduce myself and I lock up."

Lucy slid back on the bathroom counter to pull her knees to her chest. After a glance at the door, she turned back to me and asked, "Then why do you go to the effort?"

I shrugged. "Just a good habit I picked up after my father passed."

"Oh," she said. "I'm sorry, when did he pass? Back in high school? That must have been really tough."

"I'm a tough guy."

She smiled at me. "Tough enough to fight a monster, yeah. With a kitchen knife no less."

She wasn't behaving like herself. The thought that she might be a doppelganger crossed my mind, and she noticed somehow. Maybe my body stiffened. Suddenly she was looking up at me, her face so close I could see her eyes despite the darkness. "Hey, I don't think I ever thanked you for all the help you've given me."

I narrowed my eyes. "You say thanks."

She shrugged. "Those are just words, and now you've saved my life... you know, if we get out of this, I'll be sure to properly thank you."

I had ended up near her without realizing it, but I pushed her off to arm's distance. "Lucy, if I was going to abandon you, I wouldn't have gone back to fight. Calm down. I'm not going to ditch you now."

She hesitated a moment too long to be sincere. I could feel that pause of consideration before she said, "That's not what I was getting at!"

"Don't lie."

"Oh my God, you are so hung up on Mikhaila, aren't you? Do you even realize? You've saved my life twice now. Is it so strange that I want to thank you?"

The light of her phone flashlight struck her cheekbones. I could see her hair like a halo, but her eyes were shadowed and I had no idea if she was being genuine. It had only been that morning when Mikhaila had reminded me what kind of person Lucy was. I was just useful to her. "Lucy, I already said I'm not going to abandon you. If you want to thank me, do it after we're both safe."

"So, what? We just sit here?"

"Yeah, we sit here and wait until that thing leaves or until help comes."

She pulled away and put her back to the bathroom mirror. Minutes passed, and I could still hear the breathing of the monster outside. It was soft and steady. I almost started to wonder whether we could sneak by it. Lucy broke the silence. "You know, I'm acting just like high school."

"What makes you say that?" I could think of several reasons.

"It works though, you know? Kiss ass and sucking up to the right people are how you get promoted through the corporate ladder."

"If your goal was ladder climbing, you should have picked a different career. We don't really have much freedom here, you know?"

Her head thunked against the mirror. "That's why I do all the office parties and stuff. You know? All the green frosted cookies for St Patties and the tacos for Cinco de Mayo? When it comes time for raises, who do you think they're going to give them to? The eight-to-four guy who eats at his desk and keeps his head down? Or the girl that cooks food for them once in a while?"

"Very Machiavellian of you," I said, but before she could respond to the quip, the room rumbled.

3:56

Both of us leapt up. Lucy swung the beam of her flashlight around. My sopping wet shirt fell to the ground as an earthquake rocked the office building. I didn't know what to do. The cinderblock walls of the restroom were essentially a shelter for us, even if the stalls rattled until old screwheads broke off. One of the separators clattered to the floor, banging against the toilets as the shaking came to a stop.

It left my legs feeling numb as the two of us waited. I didn't know what I was even waiting for, but the shaking stopped.

I cocked my head to one side. "Do you hear that?"

"What?"

"Nothing. There's no breathing."

I couldn't hear the monster outside. I figured the earthquake might have spooked it off, but I was still wary as I stuck my head around the corner. Rather than the blinking mess of LEDs, I saw darkness and a sepia glow in the distance. It was the staircase I had found Lucy collapsed on. Her scattered purse was still at the bottom, where I had left it amid the blood.

"The building changed," I said.

"How?"

"How the hell should I know?"

"Time maybe? How long have we been here?" Lucy asked, stepping out behind me. She handed me my wet shirt as we tentatively walked down to the illuminated room below.

"Hard to say. All the clocks are stuck on five minutes to four, aren't they?"

Lucy checked her phone and said, "Interesting. Now, it's four minutes to four. Shit, are we lost again? Did all the rooms change?"

"Maybe," I said, stepping around her spilled cosmetics. Again, the bottom flights were flooded, but one door remained. The connecting room was one of the executive war rooms, the kind with floor to ceiling windows to let in the light. "Just don't rush off and trip on the stairs again."

Lucy hesitated, looking over her stuff. I thought she was going to pick some of it back up, but instead she frowned and scratched at the bandage around her head. "You know, that's what Chuck said happened to me… but I don't think I tripped. I think something hit me over the head."

I looked over the steps again. They were non-slip rubber explicitly for running down them in emergencies. Lucy's heels weren't great for running but they weren't that bad. There also wasn't any blood on the steps, only at the bottom. It made sense, but I had to correct her. "You mean, someone."

We needed to check with Chuck, see if he had seen

someone else near the stairwell. The problem was that it could have been him. Normally, that would have been my suspicion, but with doppelgangers running around, well, we had already seen that murder was on their agenda. I was pretty sure we'd never really get the chance to ask. If the three of them had already used the badge and gotten out then hopefully we could too and then it would be in the past.

There wouldn't be justice, but there wasn't evidence. The thought of trying to explain this situation to a jury made me want to laugh.

As a more immediate concern, our options on where to go were limited. The rooms felt like a deck of cards that had been picked up, shuffled, and thrown across the table once more. Given neither of us could get through a ventilation shaft, the bathroom had been a dead end. It connected to the top of the emergency stairs, which only went down one flight to one room of options.

I'd never really thought of a conference room as a crossroads. Despite that, we had three new doors to choose from. With no sign of the monster, or anyone else for that matter, I picked a door at random and pulled it open.

"Oh, thank God," I said, staring at a utility closet within.

We raided it and came up painfully short of anything good. I didn't know what I had been imagining was in a utility closet. Most of it was shelves upon shelves of soap dispenser fluid, toilet paper rolls, cleaning chemicals, mops, and so on. The mops weren't even sturdy. They were made, apparently, from the cheapest wood money could buy. A screwdriver and a strap wrench weren't going to save my life. But there was one good thing in there.

I found a five pound monkey wrench. The janitor had written "The Negotiator" onto it, which left me smirking.

Lucy ended up with nothing more than a box cutter. "At least I can stab that bitch, right?" she said, fidgeting the razor up and down.

"In any other circumstance, that would sound very wrong," I mused. Gritting my teeth and bracing myself for disappointment, I opened the next door. Disappointment was immediate. So too was confusion. My brain struggled to understand what I was looking at, until I tilted my head to one side and realized I was looking at the lobby rotated ninety degrees.

I stuck my head through, but there was no ground for me to step onto, not unless I wanted to jump nearly twenty feet straight down to the floor, which had been a wall before the scramble. We were higher up the wall than the security office. I had to stick my head through to see we were looking out of the door that should have been for the men's bathroom. Maybe if I took a running leap I could jump to the security desk and from there go down, but it would be a one way trip unless we found some rope.

It certainly was not the exit hall.

Lucy sighed. "This just won't be easy, will it?"

"We might be in a lot of trouble actually. I'm getting concerned we might not be able to reach the door out. Did you see any rope in that utility closet?"

"I think I saw like a twenty foot extension cable. Is that strong enough?"

"You'd trust your body weight to a bit of rubber and a few hairs of copper?" With a sigh of my own and slumped shoulders, I went to the other door. I couldn't even remember what had been there before, but my hope felt all time low.

I opened the last door and hot, humid air blasted me in the face. I blinked, flinching back from the extra light, and realized I was looking at the balcony. "Hey, this was connected to the way out," I said, and stepped through. I almost killed myself as soon as I put my foot down because I stepped onto a thing that rolled. I lurched, stumbled, and had to grab onto the door frame before I smacked my face into the floor.

Lucy laughed. "And we were just discussing whether I fell down the steps."

I cleared my throat. "I guess mistakes do happen," I said, and picked up what I had stepped on. It was a wooden dowel. Cheap, light, paint flaking off of it. I was pretty sure I was holding a piece of a mop handle, except it had been sawed off to about a foot long. "That's weird. Something must have happened when the others passed through."

"Come on, let's get to the door," Lucy said.

I tossed the piece aside and strode across the balcony to the door that had led to the exit hall. Beyond was our cubicle suite. I frowned at it, Lucy crossed her arms. "You know, it's an option but I have no idea whether it's a good option."

"Let's check the other door?" I proposed, and walked to the other hall door.

Once again, I almost didn't recognize what I was looking at, but for the exact opposite reason. Once I did, I bolted into the exit hall. Lucy followed behind, examining the room with slightly more confusion than I did. The door out was wrong. It didn't have the sepia glow nor the regular shine of daylight. In fact, I couldn't see through the glass at all, and the badge scanner was inert like all the others. The least they could have done was prop it open for us.

"Step back," I said, and hefted the monkey wrench up. I squeezed it tight and gave a full swing right into the glass. It shattered into a thousand pieces, scattering into the darkness beyond. I blinked, letting the crack fade from my ears. Then I pulled out my phone and lit up the darkness. My battery was still at thirty-five percent; could be worse.

Looking at the bathroom beyond made me wilt. There was no exit here.

"Bit violent, wasn't that? A plus for effort though," a woman said. She was leaning against the vending machine, arms crossed and staring at me. Sandy blond hair, sunshine yellow tank top over denim shorts, and a casual grin on her face. I didn't recognize her, neither the blonde nor the Mikhaila look-a-like, nor a co-worker.

I almost justified myself, but I asked, "Who the hell are you?"

"Does that matter?" she responded.

Lucy ratcheted her box cutter out and started towards her. "You're one of the aliens, aren't you?"

"Alien?" the woman responded, more confused than afraid. Even the sight of the box cutter a few inches in front of her nose didn't seem to phase her. "I'm not an alien."

I rested the wrench on my shoulder. "Are you with the other girls? Tanya and Morgan?"

She blinked. "Oh, in that case, yes."

Lucy grabbed her by the shirt and pressed the edge of her knife against the girl's throat. "Let us the fuck out of here you goddamn alien! You think I won't stab you?"

The woman, maybe she was a girl actually, lifted her chin up, stretching her neck to peel away from the knife unsuccessfully. "Why do you keep calling me an alien? I'm not an alien."

"Then what are you?" I asked, hoping Lucy wouldn't slip and actually slice the girl.

The girl in yellow pondered that, then snapped her fingers. "Oh, right, Morgan said that you people would know us as magical girls now!" She struck a pose with a peace sign and a stupid grin.

Lucy and I stared at her unabashed declaration. Lucy spoke deadpan. "Now I understand why they killed all those people in Salem."

"Ack! Rude! I thought witches were supposed to be back in vogue. What gives?"

I said, "Just because people will say they are Wiccan nowadays does not mean they're in vogue. Besides, everyone liked emo and goth better."

Lucy cut in. "How do we get out? You know, don't you?"

The girl shrugged. "I mean, yeah. It's not exactly a mystery. Could you stop threatening to slit my throat though? I don't want to get blood all over my shirt. Do you have any idea how long it's been since there was someone my size here?"

I glanced at Lucy, then back at the girl. That comment probably answered more than everything else so far. "You don't need to threaten her. The monster can't fit in here anyway... I was told we just had to badge out. We found a badge, the others came here and used it. Now the door is closed and we're stuck here. What gives?"

The girl looked at Lucy until the blonde took the knife

away with a huff. Then the girl shrugged. "I don't know what you want me to tell you. Badging out is how you leave. There's no rush though."

"Thanks, but I'd rather leave the monster infested death nightmare prison thing," I said.

She huffed and planted her hands on her hips. "Builder isn't a monster."

"He tried to kill us and… and have you seen it?"

"Hey, you wouldn't look so different if you missed your ticket out of here, either."

That knocked all the words from my head. Whenever it had looked at me, I had been able to tell there was something dully intelligent in the creature. I wondered if it had even bothered to chase Mikhaila and me after it killed Seamus. Had it even killed Seamus? I realized I didn't actually know if it had. Perhaps it just found the bloody body after a doppelganger killed him. Maybe Builder hadn't cared about us until Tanya ordered it to.

So, if I didn't find a badge and get out, I'd end up some teenaged witch's monstrous thrall for how long? Forever?

Or, maybe they were actually aliens and this was just part of their test.

Lucy asked, "What the hell is this place?"

The girl grinned and cleared her throat. "You see, you know how women's clothes never have pockets? It's because they've all been meticulously stolen to build this pocket dimension!" The girl's grin cracked when neither of us laughed. She wilted. "I'm sorry, that was a joke; but, it is a magic pocket dimension. What do you expect from me? A lecture? If I spent the next fifty years explaining how this place works, you wouldn't have the mind left to understand it, so I'm not gonna bother."

Lucy ratcheted her box cutter open again. "I hear spells break if you kill the spellcaster."

The girl flinched back, almost crawling up the wall to get away from her. "Just you try! I bite."

I grabbed Lucy by the arm and stopped her from trying to slash the girl's throat. "It might undo the spell, if this is a spell. Or it might trap us forever and leave us monsters without masters."

Lucy clicked her tongue. "Better a free monster than a slave."

"Save it for when we can't find a badge," I said, rising back up. I pointed the Negotiator at her and said, "Lucy, don't let her out of your sight. These girls tend to vanish, and this time, we're bringing her with us."

Lucy did not cut the girl's throat out. As it turned out, the leather bracelets she had on one wrist were genuine leather, not some kind of vegan replacement. She turned the strap into a makeshift handcuff and tied her wrist to the girl's. The disbelief in the girl's face was almost too surreal to believe.

I had no plan to climb through an elevator shaft, even if I could see light coming through from below, so we went back to our cubicle suite. "The water stopped flowing," I said, squishing some of the sodden carpet. I could hear drips falling from the paneling down to the concrete. All the electrical wiring must have been like a rainforest.

"What are we looking for?" Lucy asked, giving the girl a jerk to keep her moving along.

"I don't know. A badge out I guess."

"You gotta find the door out too," the girl in yellow said.

"So that door won't open again?"

"I dunno, maybe in the future, but not right now," she said.

I huffed. "The future, huh?" The clock in the suite also said four minutes to four. It obviously wasn't the time. We'd been in the pocket dimension for hours. I was lucky I didn't have kids, or a dog, to take care of. Ed had kids to get back to, but I was pretty sure everyone else was single like me. Maybe a dog or a cat.

I really wasn't feeling smart enough to figure this out. I had a new appreciation for why Sherlock Holmes type stories were so popular. They gave a feeling of vicarious smartness. I needed to find Mikhaila. Maybe the two of us could figure it out.

If she was still in the building.

With no other choice, I led the way. The closest door was through the closet, which had connected to the auto department. This time it was to a women's room. I glanced at Lucy, she glanced at the wannabe magical girl. Lucy asked, "You're not going to claim to need to go, are you?"

"Would you let me if I did?"

"Probably not."

"Well, it's good that I don't need to, isn't it?" the girl asked, giving her tied up wrist a shake.

I started for the next door. "Come on. And you, are you the one that made the clones?"

"You people make those, not us," she said.

Without a better idea of action, I opened the closet door and found the cafeteria. For a moment, I was apprehensive about going there, where the monster could be. Then I remembered that Chuck might not have actually escaped.

I ran forward, only slowing down when I thought I might slip on the bloody glass. The place was a mess. Tables everywhere, the tiles broken, and blood. Far more blood than a human could have. The two of us must have cut Builder more than I realized. When I went over to the mess of tables though, there was no body. If Chuck had died, it at least wasn't there.

"Ryan," Mikhaila said, walking from the shadows of the food court. She was alone, but uninjured. I let out a breath I didn't realize I had been holding and started over to her. Only then did I see the steak knife she was carrying. "Hold up," she said, lifting the weapon between us.

I lifted my hands, and glanced around. The only other people in the cafeteria were Lucy and the girl. "Yeah?"

"How do I know you're you?" she asked, her eyes dancing over me. "And why don't you have a shirt on?"

"Uh…" was not a dignified answer. Still, I held up the wet thing and said, "Because it's wet… I used it to stop a leak in the bathroom… after we got stuck in there."

"We?" she asked, eyes narrow.

"Lucy and I. We found the girl after. Do you mind putting the knife down?"

"Do you mind putting the monkey wrench down?" she countered.

After a moment of deliberation, I said, "Fair point. I guess I do mind. Can we start with what the hell happened with the badge?"

She lowered the knife but didn't put it away. "You mean

the way out? I don't know. Ed used it on the scanner, there was a flash of light, next thing I knew I was in the HR suite." She gestured to the opposite side door that we had come in from.

That gave me something to think about. My gut said that meant the badges were one time use. One badge, one person got to leave. No tailgating the door. Then, the door moved somewhere else and a different badge would be needed. The clock going down one minute seemed to coincide with that, except there had been six of us and only five minutes.

Did that imply only five people could leave? One would get stuck behind to turn into a monster?

"Uh, hey?" Lucy said. "Maybe we should talk this out somewhere safer?"

I glanced up at the broken dome, the orange mist trailing in, and nodded. A moment later, we sat down in the executive conference room. I sat the monkey wrench down on the chair next to me so I could rub my face. I thought it might take some of the confusion and fatigue out of me, but we were still in the same shit position when I opened my eyes again. "We are screwed."

Mikhaila gestured at the girl. "Can we go back to how and why you have a little girl tied up?"

"I have a name," she said.

I glared at her. "You gunna share it with us?"

She stuck her tongue out at me.

"Insurance," Lucy said. "Against the monster."

The girl stared up at her. "Don't you think it's a little silly to think calling Builder is the only thing I can do to protect myself?"

"Then why haven't you?" Lucy asked.

The girl sniffed and turned away. "Maybe I already have."

"So, to recap," I said, getting all of their attention on me, "we need to find our ID badges to get out of here. So far, we have only found one, and it was on Ed's clone. Which implies we have to find and... what? Kill? Our own clones. Is that right, Hermoine?"

She scowled at me. "Don't call me that. And, they're not clones. They are you, just a different you."

I glanced around the room but no one else seemed to get the distinction that the girl was making. Mikhaila shook her head. "I don't know about you two, but there's something weird about killing myself."

"Maybe we don't need to kill them, just get the badge off of them. But, the badge is useless without knowing where the door out is."

Lucy perked up. "Hey, wait, doesn't that mean we can use the badge to figure out who is real and who's a clone?"

Mikhaila said, "If they didn't leave the badge somewhere hidden."

I said, "We don't know that they can. If they're aliens, or doppelgangers, or whatever, maybe they were created such that they have to keep the badge. They might be like golems, you know? If the little paper thing gets taken out they no longer have instructions to follow."

Lucy said, "There's also the chance that the clones just didn't think to hide the badge."

The three of us took so long to consider the idea that the witch clapped her hands together with a grin. "Does that mean you're going to be strip searching each other?" Her gaze panned across and locked on Lucy.

I hit her in the face with my wet shirt. She collapsed in her chair like a play actor, even made some strangled sobs of death for pity points. I ignored her and stood up. First, I took off my socks and shoes, putting them on the table to show they were empty. Then I turned out my pockets. When I couldn't invert my back pockets I just took my pants off and gave them a shake. It let them all look at my boxers, but so be it.

"I got nothing. No badge," I said, doing a little turn around.

"Or you stashed it," Mikhaila countered.

I turned and frowned at her. "I think it's your turn."

Her eyebrows went up. "Excuse me?"

Lucy narrowed her eyes. "Ryan, why don't you swap weapons with her and step out for a minute? Us girls can get naked and stuff, and I'm less afraid of her with that club than with a steak knife."

And so, I put my pants back on, then we switched the leather handcuff from Lucy to me, and I walked back to our cubicle suite to wait. The girl sat on one of the printer tables, staring at the mist. I could hear the rustling of clothes as both women stripped down and ransacked each other's outfits, but I faced the mist as well.

The longer it took, the harder it was for me to see the girl as some kind of enemy. I just couldn't sense any malice from her. She hadn't even tried to escape. Maybe she was telling the truth? It wasn't like she was the one that had told the monster to kill us. I tried a different strategy. "So, do you live here, then?"

"While it lasts." She ran a finger across the railing.

"How old are you?"

She laughed. "Not a very polite question."

Chuck interjected, "Older than you, Ryan." The older man strolled in from the cafeteria, scratching his chin and carrying that gridle blade he had fought the monster with. Blood had dried onto the steel.

The girl rolled her eyes. "How completely not nice to see you again, Chuck. Kill anyone, recently?"

"Only the monster, and only tried to," he said, then he sized me up and down. "I suppose a clone wouldn't be harassing one of the game masters. Are you alone? Otherwise, I mean."

I almost answered his question, but realized there was a better idea. "Lucy is nearby. What about the others? What happened to Mikhaila and Ed?"

"Ed escaped without us. Mikhaila is right behind me. Damn building got all scrambled up again. By the time we realized the doors were different, the monster had stuck his head in to join us. Almost took my arm off before we scrambled down the elevator. It's already got our scent and frankly I don't think I'll win a fight with it, so we're trying to avoid it. Have you found the new door out? We think the way out changed during the whole mixup thing."

"Ah, shit," I said. I should have known getting teleported was too good to believe.

Lucy screamed, "Oh, you pickpocket little bitch! Ryan!"

And so, our first interrogation began. I hoped it would also be our last. We had both Mikhailas sitting next to each other in the conference room. To keep them straight, the teleported, allegedly, Mikhaila had her hair tied up while the one who had come with Chuck kept her hair down. Otherwise, they looked completely identical. I had thought I had seen differences between Ed and his clone, but now I was second guessing myself.

Chuck, Lucy, and I all kept looking between the two of them until Chuck's Mikhaila, who I had to think of as C-Mikhaila, rolled her eyes. "All you're proving right now is that none of you know what I actually look like. Even if, like, a mole was wrong, would any of you know?"

"If it was the one on your thigh, I would," I said.

Everyone looked to me as I stared at one, then the other; which was stupid. We needed to see if one was reacting differently. I didn't notice anything. Both Mikhailas took the same amount of time to remember the one beach party me and her had gone to in Junior year of high school. She'd been coaxed into wearing a slim, black bikini and everybody had taken a chance to stare. Of course I had as well, and I still remembered the little spot beneath her ass.

"Oh my god, Ryan, really?" T-Mikhaila asked.

"Sorry, it made an impression on me. Puberty and all that."

The magical girl was having fun with the situation regardless. She laughed and clapped her hands. "So are you going to make them strip?"

T-Mikhaila slammed her hands onto the conference room table. "I told you, that was Ed's card! You set me up with no way to explain. How do I even know you're the real Lucy?"

"I've been with her since we all met up at Ed's corpse." I picked up the card, turning it around. More than faded, it seemed like there had never been identifying text on it at all, but maybe I was just seeing what I expected to see. The spot that should have had a picture was rubbed off, no, it looked like it had been scraped off recently.

T-Mikhaila crossed her arms and blew some hair out of her face. "She could have been fake at that point. Maybe the real Lucy is dead in a closet somewhere."

Chuck grunted. "Unfortunately, I couldn't say whether Ed took his card with him or not, and we didn't stay long enough because of the monster. Still, I didn't get teleported after, but that just means she's the one who was with us earlier, not that she is the real one. I think we should check the mole."

C-Mikhaila sneered at him. "Don't be disgusting."

"If," I cut in, "we need to do that, I'm the only one who needs to see it. Chuck, you can step outside if it comes to that."

Chuck asked, "How do you two know each other, anyway? Are you two hooking up or something, because how would a mere co-worker–"

T-Mikhaila said, "We went to high school together."

"Oh, so you're exes or something?"

I almost answered, but C-Mikhaila spoke first. "Never more than friends." Both of the Mikhailas seemed to sink into their chairs and think about that. Lucy and Chuck, again, were looking at me. Only the witch watched the entire room, and she had a grin on her face like she was at the movies. Still, I couldn't see a difference between them.

"That was a long time ago," I said, waving off a consoling pat on the back from Chuck. I wasn't entirely sure I wanted him near me. If they had been teleported, then Chuck was a fake too. He had the weapon from earlier, but there were probably multiples of those. I stole a glance at it and examined the blood stains. It was probably the same Chuck as earlier.

That didn't mean trusting him was smart.

I jerked my hand into the air, the one tied to the game master, as Chuck had called her. "Can somebody take her? Because yeah, I think checking the mole makes sense. If that is Ed's card, then that means this Mikhaila won't have one hiding in a pocket and I can see to that too. So, how about the two of you step out?"

C-Mikhaila scanned the room and settled her eyes on T-Mikhaila. "Can't we like, quiz her memory or something? Look for a slip up?"

The witch laughed and I had to say, "That would only work if one of us knew your history well enough, and well, again, that's just me and a few memories from high school. Honestly, I'd rather check the mole than go over those details."

"You know," T-Mikhaila said, "I kind of agree with you there."

Chuck snorted. "We could just leave them a knife and let the two of them sort it out."

"No," both Mikhaila's said at once.

"Lucy, would you mind?" I said, and transferred the improvised handcuff to her. Both Mikhailas stood up as the others left the room. Part of me wondered what it said about those two that they agreed to leave me alone with both Mikhailas, but I could only focus on one problem at a time. Still though, two Mikhailas. "You know, twins are supposed to be hot, not vaguely terrifying."

C-Mikhaila snorted as she walked around the table,

tugging her shirt out from her skirt. "Tell that to the twins from *The Shining*."

"Never watched it."

"How?"

"I don't like horror movies."

"But like, nobody likes horror movies. People watch them as a… Oh."

I grimaced. "Yeah, I didn't have a girlfriend to take to scary movies."

"Point taken," she said, and unbuttoned her bottoms. She turned around and huffed. Then she dropped her skirt to the ground and slid her leggings down. I got to see her panties, but I wasn't in the right mindset to even take a mental snapshot. It wasn't the first time I had seen her like that. I just watched as the waist of her pants slipped down to her thighs.

"It's there," I said, and she pulled them right back up. She was still pulling her skirt back up as we both turned to T-Mikhaila.

She sighed and walked over on the other side of me. She repeated the process with the exact same mannerisms, and had the exact same mole in the same spot. Just a little brown dot, easy to miss.

I sighed. "Well, there goes that," I said, and like my words triggered it, the door to the staircase, not where Chuck and Lucy had taken the girl, opened. T-Mikhaila almost fell over in the process of yanking her skirt back up while Tanya, the first one who looked like a teenaged Mikhaila, strolled inside with a shit eating grin.

I jumped up. "Grab her."

Tanya held out her hand. "Hold on, you don't want a fight.

You want my help, right?" she said, showing us Mikhaila's badge.

C-Mikhaila clicked her tongue. "So she stashed it?"

"So the other badge was Ed's?" I asked.

T-Mikhaila circled round as she buttoned her skirt. "No, I think we should still grab her."

"Ah, ah, ah," Tanya said, leaping up on one of the chairs, then onto the table with a grin. "I'm the only one who can tell you which is which!"

The Mikhailas, in unison, said, "We know which is the real one!" C-Mikhaila added, "And why do you look like I used to?"

"Because I can," Tanya answered, smirking back at her.

I picked up the Negotiator, slow and deliberately. "If you even think of calling that monster again, I'm caving your skull in."

The girl snickered. "Oh, how scary. Can I ask you a question though?"

I narrowed my eyes. "Shoot."

"Why does it matter which is the real one?"

The three of us were at a loss for words, until T-Mikhaila said, "Because the badges are one use only. They get wiped when someone escapes. So, if the copy uses the badge, then something… inhuman will get out and we won't."

"Not very inhuman if you can't tell them apart," the girl said, not taking her eyes off me.

"While we're in here, maybe," C-Mikhaila said.

I said, "We haven't ruled out that we can't tell them apart yet."

Tanya tossed me the badge. "I'll just tell you that the clones aren't perfect–"

"So you do know what's going on."

Tanya rolled her eyes. "The only thing different between these two are their memories, and I just love that you're the only one who can judge between the two of them. So don't you have a question to ask them? A very important memory you all remember clearly? Come on now, magic has logic to it, don't you know? You think I look like this by chance?"

She looked the way Mikhaila had the day she rejected me. I glanced at the two Mikhailas. Both of them glanced away from me. I considered braining the girl anyway, but if she wanted to call in that monster again, I didn't know what I could do. Builder would kill us all. I wasn't very fast on the clever questions either; nothing came to mind as I looked over Mikhailas badge. So I played along. "Do you remember when I asked you to Homecoming?"

I looked at C-Mikhaila first. "Yes."

"Where was it?"

"Behind the school, on the track to the tennis courts. You came running over from the bike locks." That had been the only place I could catch her alone. The last thing I had wanted was public pressure.

I turned to T-Mikhaila. "What day of the week was it?"

"It was the Tuesday before Homecoming, which really put a lot of pressure on the whole thing, you know?" Because I hadn't worked up the courage earlier.

Back to C-Mikhaila. "Do you remember what you said to me?"

I couldn't read the expression she put on, but it was

obviously painful. "I mocked you for asking so close to the day." She had.

I stifled my own emotions about the matter. Now wasn't a time to be emotional. "Precisely, please."

She looked away and said, "I asked you if you really thought a girl like me didn't already have a date. But that was because it was only a few days away! Could you imagine trying to get a dress in like two days?"

"Oh, that's a lie," T-Mikhaila said. "I already had a dress."

"You did, I saw the pictures. What color was it?"

"Green," they both said.

T-Mikhaila locked eyes with me. "She got that wrong! Didn't she?"

"She didn't say she didn't have a dress," I said. She was justifying herself. "Come on, we're not kids. You were insulted a random guy like me, who you hardly knew, asked you out at the eleventh hour. It's fine. We all know if you had said yes you wouldn't have been able to go to the dance at all." Because that had been the week my father had died.

C-Mikhaila sighed. "I didn't reject you, Ryan. Not explicitly."

That gave me pause. It dragged me right out of the pit of memory. "No, you definitely rejected me," I said, and glanced to T-Mikhaila. She didn't leap on the opportunity to prove herself.

C-Mikhaila finally looked me in the eyes. "I scolded you, I didn't reject you. I asked what you were thinking asking me out to Homecoming when you hadn't asked me out before."

"Yeah, that sounds like a rejection to me."

She groaned. "I'm sorry, Ryan. I was stupid back then, okay? I thought you would get it!"

"Get what? You shot me down and I never talked to you again. That was a rejection. And hell, that's a two way street. You didn't say another word to me until we realized we were working at the same company."

T-Mikhaila shuffled her feet, edging away from me. "What I meant, back then, the real me, was you should have asked me out sooner and I would have said yes. I couldn't believe it took you all the way until Homecoming. I was... upset about it, and childish."

"Hold on," I said. "That's fucking bullshit. One of you is lying. You've gotta be."

Neither of them accused the other of lying. Tanya had to grab her belly as she threw her head back and laughed at us.

I threw my free hand in the air. "Well ain't this just fucking great. Both have the same mole and the same memories. Fan-fucking-tastic. Lovely way to learn I screwed the pooch in high school, ain't it? This just makes it so much easier to escape this nightmare."

Tanya stifled her laughter long enough to ask, "Can you spot the difference yet?"

I forced a smile and glared at her. "I'm about ready to take Chuck's suggestion and leave them in a closet with a knife and just take whoever survives. You fucking lied to me, didn't you? Lie by omission."

"Oh?" the girl responded, tilting her head and grinning.

"Their memories are different by technicality, aren't they? Different since the moment the copy was made. I bet everything about their past is a perfect duplication but the last few hours are different."

The girl shrugged. "Maybe, maybe not. As a reward though, I'll tell you that's not the only difference. And who knows, you might like the copy better!"

C-Mikhaila stepped forward and said, "Ryan, I still like you, okay?"

"Woah!" T-Mikhaila said, putting up her hands and backing up to the wall. "That has nothing to do with memories. That's not even accurate. I assure you I had boyfriends through college. That clone is just playing on your emotions to make you side with her."

C-Mikhaila stepped closer. "Why do you think I was harping on you today about bending over for Lucy? I was jealous!"

I held up my hand to stop her. "Alright, I've heard enough. You're the fake," I said, pointing at C-Mikhaila. "There's no fucking way the real Mikhaila would say any of that."

Tanya walked across the table and leaned over to grin at me. "That's where the fun is," she said. "You're the judge. You're the one that will decide which is real and which isn't. Who gets to leave and who stays behind. So, which will it be? Do you want to take the Mikhaila who likes you? The one still as hung up on you as you are on her? Or the one who moved on with her life, but just feels more authentic to you? Whatever that means."

I excused myself from the conference room and walked out on the balcony. Lucy and Chuck had taken opposite ends, and I trudged between the two of them. They both looked to me expectantly, but I didn't say anything as I walked over to the railing and climbed onto it. Dangling my feet off the side, I sat down and stared at the smoke.

"Let me see, let me see," the unnamed witch said as she dragged Lucy over to the conference room door and peered inside. The two Mikhailas had taken opposite seats across the table, the Negotiator between them. Tanya had headed up the stairs when I turned my back on the problem, leaving the room idle.

Chuck walked up behind me. "Did you figure it out?"

"No," I said, peering into the sepia haze. I tried to spot the horizon, but nothing existed beyond the building. I couldn't even make out the water. It seemed higher up now, than the first time I had found the balcony.

"So, what are we going to do?"

"I don't know. Find the exit first, I guess. If we can use someone else's badge then we can at least know–well at least I will know–whether the people in the room get teleported. I guess you're obligated to assume your Mikhaila is the real one, right?"

Chuck leaned against the railing with crossed arms. "Like I said, if the one with me is fake, she might have just been fake the whole time. I'll restrain myself from forcing the matter until we demonstrate that badging out doesn't teleport any-one. As for finding the exit though, the two of us will have to do that together, in case that monster shows up again."

"I'm not so sure we have to worry about the monster," I said. "As long as we're entertaining these girls, they won't need to spice it up."

Chuck didn't say anything for a while. "Did you learn something?"

"Do you think we're in a dream?" I asked. The water was at least four stories beneath me. I wondered if I would die if I fell to it.

"I think at most one of us is in a dream. You can't be in someone else's dream, right? Everyone else would have to be figments of your imagination."

"Maybe," I said. "Ancient people thought the gods revealed themselves to mortals through dreams though. So, at least the girls might be real."

"They're not gods."

"How can you be sure?"

"I guess I'm not."

"Don't you find it strange that the clones, the doppelgang-ers or whatever–"

"Figments of regret," the girl said. We all turned to her as she smirked at me. "You know, like, most people, most of the time, they're not even really awake. Their present moment is sort of just a blob of preprogrammed responses to stimuli. Their dreams and desires are muted and fuzzy at best and they just get through the day. That's why so many people can just rewatch the same episodes of Officefield over and over and over again." I wondered if she was intentionally getting show names wrong. "You couldn't replicate somebody like that no matter how hard you tried. But for a human? A moment of regret? That's like a snapshot of existence burned into them. No, more like an engraving for a woodblock. You can just plop it down and duplicate it."

"You're really not sounding like a magical girl," I said. She flinched back, speechless, as I turned back to the fog. If her explanation was right, it did make it all feel like a dream. Of course I could dream up a fake Mikhaila with a fake regret like that.

"Oh, yeah?" Lucy asked, free hand on her hip. "Then what was Ed's regret?"

"You mean the mild mannered office worker who didn't even flinch from caving in the skull of his copy? I'll give you a hint, his regret is buried in the woods four feet deeper than a deer carcass on the north branch of Shashta Lake just out of sight from a carpool parking lot."

Chuck groaned. "God damn it. I knew that guy was a psychopath. At least he's away from us now."

I had just thought he was a psycho because management always felt that way and I didn't know anything about his life. Greeting him was a hell of a thought to look forward to after escaping this place. I had Mikhaila's badge in my pocket. I could feel the plastic against my thigh. I wondered if I could use it to get out of here myself, leave them to deal with it and sort out who the real Mikhaila was. I suspected I could only use my own badge to use the door though.

"If this were a dream," I said, glancing at Chuck. "How would you wake up?"

He cocked an eyebrow at me. "Other than realizing it? That usually pulls me out. Have you tried plugging your nose and breathing?"

I plugged my nose. I couldn't breathe through it. I sighed. "That would just alert you that you're dreaming. That's a lucid dreaming trick, right?" I'd read about it years ago in college, never pulled it off to my knowledge though. But, maybe I had these kinds of dreams every night and simply forgot them in the morning. I knew that sometimes dreams felt like they never ended. There was another way to check, and I was facing it.

Chuck glanced over the edge. "I'd appreciate it if you didn't test the hypothesis… Like I said, there's a monster out there. I could use your help."

"But, what if you're just part of the dream, trying to keep me here and torture me?"

"How would you dream of somebody you'd never met before?"

I frowned. "I don't know, maybe I have met you before and I forgot." I peered over the edge. Four stories into water. I wondered if the surface tension would kill me, or if I'd just plunge in like an action movie.

"Well, think about it this way. If this is a dream, how do you know jumping would actually kill you to wake you up? If it's dream logic, the water will just catch you. Or maybe another monster will snatch you safely, or something. And if it's not a dream, that's game over for you, and likely for us too."

I sighed and buried my face in my hands. "I don't know what to do, man."

"Hey, you," Lucy said, shaking the girl's arm. "Shouldn't you be saying something here?"

"Like what?" the girl responded. "If he wants to jump off and kill himself, who am I to stop him?"

"He's not trying to die! He's trying to escape."

"Death is a form of escape, isn't it? You might even say it's the courageous choice. Or the virtuous choice. Clones they may be, but your copies think and feel just like you do. It's murder of a form. And would you stop–" The strand holding

Lucy's wrist to the girl's snapped. The cord fell to the ground between them and everyone took a breath to process.

The magical girl bolted, ducking under Lucy's arm and darting for the cafeteria. Chuck and Lucy scrambled to catch her. I was still pulling my legs over the balcony railing when something caught my eye. I wouldn't have ever seen it if I hadn't been distracted, but there were things in the water below me. More than just vague blocks that emerged from the water, I saw Builder walking between them. The scale made it click together in my mind. I was looking at skylights. Not just any skylights, but the ones that were outside my work suite. Part of the wonderful cityscape I was treated with was the gravel roof overtop the bottom floor sprawl around the tower.

If skylights were sticking out from the water, then there was a room beneath the water. The moment I realized that, Builder seemed to sense me, and lifted its serpentine neck to stare at me.

I fell off the railing, hitting the tile floor of the balcony hard. C-Mikhaila stepped out as I groaned. She had the Negotiator. "What happened?"

"The girl ran. Come on, we have to find the way out," I said, taking the wrench from her.

T-Mikhaila followed a moment later, glaring at her copy, and the three of us jogged into the cafeteria. We found Lucy panting against the wall, holding a hand to her bandaged head. She sheepishly gestured to the left, around the fight wreckage. "Chuck went on. I'm… a bit light headed to be running."

"You need food," I said.

"I'm not hungry."

Neither was I. "Doesn't matter, eat. Mikhailas, one of you stay and help her, alright?"

T-Mikhaila shook her head. "Not while you have my badge. Are you going to give that back or not?"

I stopped, one step to follow Chuck, and looked at her. "Give it back? When did you have it?"

She didn't get embarrassed. Her eyes just half closed as she glared at me. "Really? Word games?"

I stared back at her, not getting a flicker of falsity from her. Then I asked myself a question. If the doppelgangers started with the cards, why didn't they just leave in the first place? Either it had been mere coincidence, which perhaps it had–we still hadn't found my clone–or, they couldn't leave with the cards. Maybe they had to kill the original or something. "Here," I said, handing her the badge as I furrowed my brow and looked at her.

She checked to see it was her own card, then squeezed her hand into a fist around it. "Thank you," T-Mikhaila said, and turned her attention to Lucy and C-Mikhaila. "Come on, you need more food and water."

"No, you're coming with me and she's staying," I said, grabbing T-Mikhaila by the arm before jogging in the direction Chuck had gone. The left hand passage from the cafeteria went into the HR suite, which was level once more. The carpet squelched underfoot, water still draining out of it, but I could see Chuck standing at the coffee station door. We had come in from the middle, and soon saw what had stopped him.

The door beyond was a direct drop from the top of the lobby. "She jumped," he said, gesturing over the edge.

I peered and didn't see a corpse. "So, she can fly or something?"

"Or something. I was still catching up when she jumped and then she was just gone."

"Funny how they can do that."

Chuck sighed and nodded at T-Mikhaila. "So, did you figure out which is which?"

She glanced at me expectantly, and I nodded. "Yeah, I know which is which."

"Well, that's one problem fixed. We still need to find the way out though."

"Plenty of doors to check. Builder is out of the way too. Let's split up," I said, and took T-Mikhaila's hand in my own. She squeezed it back, falling in behind me as I headed across the suite. Chuck trailed us and split off at the second hall door. The server room was beyond that, and he went in to check the other doors. I took T-Mikhaila down to the utility closet door.

"Thank you," she said.

"For what?"

"Believing me. God, I should have apologized to you so long ago. I was young and stupid and didn't realize why you suddenly got so distant. I thought it was because of me and shit, our lives could have gone so differently!"

I pushed the door open and found our suite beyond. I let my breath out and started striding to the emergency fire escape. "Let's focus on the current issue first," I said, passing our desks. "We need to find the way out, and we have to find my clone so I can get my badge to leave."

"Okay? That's fine? Ryan, where are you going?"

When I had first woken up, I hadn't thought about going out into the smoke, not until the open window in the cafeteria. It had seemed dangerous, like monsters would be lurking in it. I laughed when I found the door was stuck shut. I figured it was probably something to do with the electronic alarms, something about the twisting of the building, but it was just a door. I smashed the glass apart with the Negotiator. Shards of broken glass sprayed across the water outside as a dirty tide poured into the suite. An inch of dull water poured across our feet as I knocked out the last of the glass pane. "This way," I said.

T-Mikhaila blinked and gaped at me as I crawled out. She followed me as I strolled out among the skylights. The roof was fairly large, at least as big as the cafeteria. One edge even bordered against the broken glass dome. I could see where Builder had climbed up and fallen through to attack us. "Ryan, what are you doing out here? We need to find a door, not just go swimming. Are you crazy?"

I walked all the way to the lip of the roof, the half foot of masonry that retained the gravel. Water poured in through the rain gutters, constantly filling the roof and flowing across, back to the suite and into the building. There were no doors on the roof, but there were skylights. I turned back to T-Mikhaila because I wasn't looking for the way out.

I nodded. "Well, I want to say it's good to know I wasn't wrong to ask you out back then. You know, for years I did wonder if I was just some kind of mistaken idiot, because I was sure you'd say yes."

"I should have!"

I walked back over to her. When she lifted her gaze to meet mine, I asked, "What if I asked you now?"

"Asked me what?"

"If I asked you out now, would you say yes?"

She bit her lip and nodded. When I leaned down, she leaned up on her toes and the two of us kissed. Some ten years in anticipation, and I finally got to kiss my high school crush. It made me want to cry as I slipped my hand into her pocket. "Do you remember when the two of us were hiding from the monster?"

"What about it?"

"I was really impressed when you used that cup to check the water level. I didn't want to admit it, but I was panicking. The fact you kept a level head… it's one of the things I like about you."

She blushed and fidgeted. "Thanks, Ryan. We really need to find the way out of here though. Shouldn't we keep going?"

I stepped back from her with a shake of my head. She saw the change in my expression: the pain. "That was a lie." Then I finally felt the tremble in the floor. It was muted by the water, but the closer it got, the more I could feel the reverberations. Of course, I had been the one to use the cup. The clone had all the memories of Mikhaila from before we got here, and maybe a slightly different perspective on our past, but she didn't know what had happened in here.

T-Mikhaila was the fake, and if I needed any more evidence–I had to admit it was possible the first Mikhaila had been fake the whole time—Builder emerged from the mist. It walked up behind her, looming around her like she wasn't even there. Its attention was only on me.

Of course the monsters of this place wouldn't fight each other.

The fake Mikhaila stamped her foot on the ground, baring her teeth at me as she shouted, "You just wait until I find your badge! Until I find your clone and rob you of your chance to escape! You hear me?"

I took the Negotiator and smashed open the nearest skylight. Builder pulled back, surprised by the noise it seemed. His eyes were tiny and glossy, almost buried in folds of hide that I could only makeout now that I was but a few feet from him. If he could see me, he was as blind as a twenty year old dog. It was the fake Mikhaila who made a grab for me, but I dove through the skylight.

Beneath the roof was another room, but I couldn't see anything. There was no light to speak of because the room was completely submerged. The water wasn't cold but body temperature, like a bath. The wrench weighed me down, slowing me as I pumped and kicked. The only thing I could see was another splash of light, one not blocked by my own body. I went up and broke through the surface. In the dome of another skylight, I sucked in fresh breath.

Then I shoved my head under water. Through the distortion in my ears, I heard the crash and break of the first skylight. Metal and glass dropped into the water, trailing bubbles. I saw Builder's foot stick through before it pulled back, leaving the opening agape. But that made it easier for me to see the room beneath the water.

It was the corporate amphitheater. I should have guessed purely by the size of the roof, hardly anything else could line up with it. Rows of chairs like sunken tombstones arrayed beneath me, the room had one set of doors out. I was thankful I had been fighting to hold onto the Negotiator, because when I started swimming down, it dragged me to the floor. A few hops across the bottom and I threw my shoulder to the doors out.

Water pressure did the rest. Like I had been grabbed by the fist of God, I was thrown forward and slammed into a cubicle wall. The supports at the bottom snapped off, knocking it over and throwing me with it. I almost didn't realize my head was above water as I tumbled across the cubicle suite. The further I got from the door, the weaker the flow became and the moment I could, I scrambled atop a filing cabinet and looked around. I was in the auto claims suite.

I started coughing and gagging, spitting out water that had gotten in my lungs. My whole body hurt from the ordeal, like I had been hit by football linebackers. The water didn't slow down just because I was in pain though. The whole suite was slowly going to flood from the gushing water. I had come in from one of the hall doors, which left another hall door, the coffee station, and the closet.

Scrambling from desk to cabinet and over again, like a kid playing The Floor Is Lava, I bolted for the next hall door. I had to jump into the water to pull it open, and almost lost my footing. I managed to rip the door open to steady myself, and found a utility closet beyond. I swore. A vacuum cleaner wasn't going to help me.

Climbing onto the printer table, and then once more

across the cubicles, I ran for the coffee station. The building's lack of electrical power was surprisingly lucky at the moment, and I caught a glimpse of a wall clock as I ran. Still four minutes to four. The water was only ankle deep all the way at the end of the suite, and I was able to throw the door open. I almost didn't recognize the room beyond–just a blank wall a few feet across from me. There was a hallway to either side. I was looking at a cubby that had nothing but a faucet. To my surprise, the door had actually opened up correctly: I was looking at the main hall of the tower.

There should have been a vending machine like the one outside my suite, but apparently the auto team just wasn't as highly valued or something. "Shit, where do I go?" Water still poured around my feet, flowing from the suite and into the hall. The utility closet wasn't going to absorb the flow, and neither would the cubicles. That entire torrent would eventually be pouring out this door if I didn't find a way to drain it back out. I needed a–

Cursing myself for an idiot, I turned around and waded across to the floor-to-ceiling windows. Using the Negotiator once more, I hammered the glass. The wrench bounced off, reverberating the pane. My hands stung, but not like when I had struck the exit. The glass was just tough. The second blow cracked it and the third made a spiderweb. The fourth shattered the pane and let the mist in.

I shut the door between the suite and the hall and leaned against it. Finally able to take a breath, I almost slid down to the ground in a heap. I would have, if the ground had been dry. I could hear the tinkling of water down the elevator shafts. The hall wasn't large. It was vaguely shaped like a dumbbell, with a conference room at one end and the elevator stack at the other. There was no balcony access, which meant I was on one of the top floors, but the hall was sandwiched between two suites–plenty of doors to check. I paced around, shook my head at the collaboration zone, and rounded the corner to the elevators. One of the doors was rotated ninety degrees, laid flat across the ground.

When I pried the noisy, vertical, one open, I found the bottom of an elevator shaft beyond. I couldn't even climb, because the elevator box was directly overhead. Water just dripped over the edge and fell into the pit.

So I pried open the door on the other elevator. The vertical lobby laid beyond, but this time with only a short drop to the bottom wall. I nodded, but didn't go through. There were too many other doors to check in the hall. Part of me wondered just how large the construct could be, possibly as large as the entire office building, but that would have included dozens of cubicle suites. I didn't even know what most of them looked like. Other companies rented entire floors from the tower, completely unrelated to the company that we all worked for.

I was wondering if that was some kind of clue, a bound on the size of the dimension, when I checked one of the suite doors. The hall had an enormous amount of connections. From the perspective of looking for the exit, it was a windfall. Naturally, to balance out this luck, the doors almost entirely opened to dead end conference rooms. I almost got my hopes up when I realized the men's restroom opened to a women's restroom, and vice versa across the hall. Then I found a door that wouldn't open.

The handle rattled in the frame and I saw a badge scanner blinking red.

I felt like scum, knowing that I had used the kiss to steal Mikhaila's badge back. It was in my hand, ready to be scanned. I could probably badge out and leave right then, but then what? I'd be gone, like Ed was gone. Mikhaila, the real one, as well as Lucy and Chuck, would still be trapped in here with a monster.

Instead, I tried my luck with the wrench. The impact was like striking granite instead of a flimsy office door. The impact bounced back through my wrists and numbed my hands until I nearly dropped the wrench. I wondered if maybe the badge scanner could be snapped off, but I was too afraid we'd be stuck forever if I did that.

So, I went to the elevator and climbed through. I turned my head up to all the doors overhead and I screamed, "I found the exit!" Of course, there was no way to know who would hear me or who would get to me first. It wasn't exactly easy to descend the lobby. I couldn't even think of what they could use as a rope. A braid of ethernet cables maybe? That could take them hours to make.

Someone else found me first. Morgan said, "You really made a mess."

I almost fell out the elevator door before I spun around to face her. "Where the hell did you come from?"

She glanced around, counted the doors, and nodded. "I think you stopped one door short of checking the emergency exit?"

"There's no way–damn it, I did, didn't I?"

She laughed. "For as clever as you were to get out to

the amphitheater like that... what, did you use up all your cleverness?"

I sighed and walked over to her. She didn't step back, so I didn't feel the need to handcuff her like the other girl. "Give me a break, I'm tired. Probably half-starved and I just haven't felt it yet."

She smiled and tilted her head at me, then out from her pocket she produced a flaccid candy bar. The chocolate had melted, folding over in the middle. "Need a snack?"

I couldn't imagine something less appetizing at the moment. I was still dripping wet and half clothed. The surrealness sank in as I stood there in front of a little girl like a caveman. I even had a club. "Not really hungry."

She didn't react. "Haven't you been in here a long time?"

"Feels like four hours, maybe five. I haven't been able to keep track."

"And you're not hungry?"

"Adrenaline does that to you."

After a moment, she shrugged and tossed it aside. "So, I've gotta know. Why are you certain you know which Mikhaila is the real one?"

"How much do you know about her?"

She shrugged. "Not much. I don't know much about you either." And yet Tanya had implied she knew where Ed had buried a corpse? That didn't fit right with me.

"Mikhaila and I have been working together for a few years now. Even if she did regret turning me down when she didn't mean to, it's been too long for her to apologize. Humans don't just break down one day and confess, not when they've been holding it in."

"That sounds silly to me."

"If they did, they'd be admitting that all that time they held back was a mistake. The… compulsion to hide mistakes is very… very strong."

"That's stupid though."

"You're not human, are you?"

Morgan's face was blank, then became a new kind of smirk. She stood up straight, put her hands on her hips, and said, "No, we're not."

"So, are you aliens? Or magical girls? Or–"

"Gods?"

"Something like that, yeah."

"Something like that indeed, as far as you're concerned. Is there a difference though?"

"It's the rules of the game I want to understand. Do we really get to leave if we badge out?"

She nodded. "If you do, you'll wake up like this never even happened. So, good luck finding your regret and overcoming it."

"Where the hell is it?"

She shrugged. "It's a big building. It's somewhere out there. I wish you the best of luck. Do me a favor though?"

It was my turn to tilt my head. "What?"

"Be careful who you trust?"

"Can I trust you when you say that?"

Morgan laughed.

Then I heard Chuck shout, "Ryan, that you down there?" His voice echoed in through the elevator door and I made the mistake of looking away from her. When I turned back, she was gone.

Chuck hollered down, "Settle in for a bit of a wait, it's a long fall and cables don't support much weight. We're gunna need a lot."

I spent the intervening time trying to find Morgan. I couldn't open the door to the flooded suite, so the only place I could check was the emergency staircase Morgan had allegedly come in from. This wasn't the one story staircase Lucy had gotten hurt on. That one was for the auxiliary building between the cafeteria and the towers. This one zig-zagged all ten floors of the tower. As per code, each tower in the building, including the one that our company had nothing to do with, had two emergency staircases, reaching all the way from top to bottom, ten floors total.

It finally made me start estimating just how large this world was, if it truly did unravel. There were at least forty cubicle suites, as many bathrooms, closets, and conference rooms. I couldn't even keep the count of doors straight in my head there were so many, and that wasn't counting everything in the lobby, cafeteria, and executive wings.

We had been idiots to not bring pencil and paper, to not draw out a map and systematically eliminate the possibilities. The fact we had stumbled into the exit twice was nothing short of a miracle, or it had been contrived that way. The unnamed girl, I really had to pick a name for her or something, had escaped this way. It was possible she had given us a hint in doing so.

It was also possible we weren't dealing with the entire building. Maybe parts had been pulled away for other people to explore. There really wasn't a reason to think only the five of us had been abducted. One of the rules of statistics was to always assume the result you got was an average result. I hadn't passed the math classes to be an actuary, but I knew that much.

Still, when I tried one of the doors and saw more stairs, I realized I had no way of knowing which of the four emergency staircases I was in–possibly all of them. Instead, I stayed in the one that connected to the exit hall, and went all the way to the bottom. The first floor was flooded, the door relatively inaccessible. That was the only scrap of information I brought back with me.

I figured their work upstairs would take at least an hour, so I sat down in the only dry seat I had available, a toilet stall. I was no stranger to killing time in a stall, but I was used to having my smart phone. The company kept the stalls professional too, it wasn't a school bathroom or something. I didn't have decades of graffiti and carvings to browse as I sat there, which left me nothing to occupy my mind until bit by bit, fatigue creeped over me.

I hadn't felt tired, just like I hadn't felt hungry. As far as my body was concerned, the clocks were accurate and no time was passing. But I had been thinking a lot, so my mind was another matter. Given the option of rest, I blacked out. The dripping of water into the elevator shaft was like a metronome, an echo of noise from the hall that faded into my dreamless sleep.

I woke up not to the sounds of footsteps, but to no sound at all. The realization I had nodded off made me jerk. I almost didn't understand the absence of the noise; but, when I shifted my feet, there was water on the tiles. The others hadn't joined me yet. With no clocks and no sun, I had no idea how long I had been sleeping, only that my legs hurt. I found that the water had filled the bottom of the elevator shaft, so at least a few hours had passed. Just to be sure, I checked that the exit was still there, then I stuck my head into the lobby and shouted again, "Are you still coming?"

There was no response.

"Hey, did something happen?"

Something had definitely happened. I hadn't actually explained which was the real Mikhaila either, I had just told them to meet me down here. If they weren't on their way to me, then I had to be on my way to them. I just didn't have a good way to find them. I had the option of swimming against the current, probably drowning, and backtracking to where Builder had been. I could also get lost in the staircase. I chose the final option, and climbed through the elevator door to the lobby. The drop to the slanted wall-turned-floor. I managed to not sprain an ankle landing, and skittered to the bottom of the room where the doors to the cafeteria were supposed to be. I found the set of double doors upright, merged into the floor, and the push bar didn't want to budge.

I thought that was weird, but also that the frame had probably shifted from the movement. The doors from the lobby were all security reinforced, since that was the most logical way for someone to break in and shoot up the place. The office building had been built well after active shooters had become a concern, so the doors were heavy. I should have been able to budge the latch though. Even my entire body weight couldn't wiggle it.

I thought perhaps it was another exit out, but there was no badge scanner. Still not convinced, I gave it a whack with the

Negotiator. The surface dented, unlike the confirmed exits. The noise it made was wrong somehow. Then I noticed the water trickling in through the frame.

I ran from it as soon as I realized the other side was submerged. The one experience of urban white water rapids was enough for one lifetime. Figuring they probably connected to the other amphitheater doors, I completely put them out of mind and ran for the security office door Mikhaila and I had used to get to the HR suite. This time, it connected to the server room.

"Mother fucker." Chuck had known from the start how to get to me. Whatever had happened must have happened before I even fell asleep. They hadn't even gathered up cables to make the rope. I tried to run through scenarios in my head of what happened, and ruled out Builder attacking them. I would have heard the noise. The only thing I could think of was that another clone had appeared. The most likely one was my own. They had no other reason to doubt me that I had found the exit, especially after I apparently sided with a fake Mikhaila.

Through the server room I went back to the auto suite, back to the cafeteria. "Hey, where is everyone?" I shouted, crossing the battlefield.

A pan clattered in one of the kitchens. I ran for it, and heard a female swearing. It wasn't Lucy or Mikhaila that I cornered, but the unnamed witch. She snarled at me, half a donut sticking out from her lips as she crouched down to sprint. The kitchen had two exits. There was the one I had used to get into the kitchen from the service counter, and to my left was a door that normally led to the utility hall, where the companies brought their food in from. She was in the deep end of the kitchen, between the stoves and storage shelves, with no way out.

"You eat stale donuts?"

She ripped the dry pastry off with one hand. After a few chews, she packed her mouthful into one cheek and said, "Yeah? What's it to you? Do you know how long it's been since I've had sugar? I miss it!"

I tried to remind myself that she was the one who had trapped us in here, but where was the danger? The malice? "I found the way out."

"Yeah? Good for you."

"Where's Mikhaila? I left her back here with Lucy."

The girl planted her hands on her hips and turned away from me. "Why should I tell you?"

I reached into my pocket and pulled out the melted chocolate bar Morgan had given me. "You want sugar, right?"

"Lucy is unconscious in the Mexican food kitchen," she said, jumping over to me with eyes locked onto the candy.

"She's what?"

"I told you now–"

I tossed the chocolate to her and ran out of the kitchen before she had even caught the chocolate. I found Lucy on the ground in front of the deep fryer. She had her head propped up against it, but her bandage was missing. "Lucy, are you alright?"

She mumbled as I knelt next to her, and I immediately checked the wound. It was just like I had found her at the start of this mess except it wasn't bleeding anymore. There was no blood flow to it at all apparently. "Ryan?" she asked.

"What happened?" I checked her pulse. Her neck was warm and her heartbeat steady. She just wasn't bleeding out of an open head wound.

"I thought you were with Mikhaila?"

"No, remember? I left her to help you. I knew you were anemic."

She grabbed my arm and squinted up at me. "No, I remember that. You came back and left with her."

"Shit," I said. I brushed my hair back, finding it still damp and knotted from my swim. "When you saw me that time, did I have this?" I asked, holding up the Negotiator.

She scrunched up her face and looked at it in the dark. "Oh, shit."

"Oh, shit indeed. Come on. We have to find them. Can you walk?"

She nodded, and I eased her up to her feet. She was more steady than I expected, but when I turned to lead her out, she stopped me. "Ryan, I think we're dead." She was staring at my feet.

"We're not dead yet."

"No, I think we died and this is hell."

I reflexively laughed. "Then where's the brimstone and fire? Come on." I pulled her on, but as soon as she saw the windows, she stopped and pointed.

"There's smoke, isn't there? And all the magic?"

"Could be dream logic."

"Ryan, no one would dream that all the computers were replaced by notebooks."

She had a good point. "Could be an alien simulation."

"Ryan, I don't think we're getting out of here."

"Oh, come on. If this were the afterlife, where's everyone else? There's no afterlife I know of that's empty smoke. A building in an ocean."

She stayed defiant. "There's oblivion."

"That's not an afterlife."

"Maybe this is just our brains having a frantic dream as we die and that's our future out there. A world where the water is below but the land hasn't been separated from the sky above. Nothing but treading water until we finally drown."

"Come on Lucy, now you're…" She was sounding like one of the clones. She wasn't bleeding either. She was the one living by dream logic, not me. "Hey, remember what you said to me when we got out of the bathroom? About the stairs."

"That I didn't slip?"

"When you said that, I figured it was somebody else out there that attacked you. Do you think it was your clone?"

"I don't know. I don't remember getting hit. Just like you don't remember how you got here."

"Come on, I want to check something," I said, keeping one eye on her as I left the cafeteria. I didn't go looking for Mikhaila, not quite. I didn't know where she was. But I did know where Ed's clone was.

I was kicking myself for not investigating this better. I had been naive to ignore the corpse. Squeamish about death in a life-and-death situation. I should have known that I was only hurting myself by shying away from it.

The auto suite was connected to our suite by means of the coffee station. The water had drained into the floor paneling, leaving the carpet only mildly wet. All the water should have diffused the blood from the body everywhere. I should have seen red staining ten feet away from it, but I didn't.

"How did we know this was the clone?" I asked, kneeling down and getting my hands on the body. Ed had caved the skull in with a landline. I could see the rectangular imprint. Most of the skin had torn off and I could see shards of bone sticking out from the pink flesh within.

"He had the badge, right?"

"Did he? Or did the other Ed put it there?"

"I don't know. How could we possibly know that?"

"That's my point. There is no difference between us and our clones," I lied. "I think the only evidence we have that Ed was the real Ed was the fact that he killed his clone. The fake Mikhaila didn't immediately try to murder the other one."

"That's because Mikhaila wouldn't kill somebody. Maybe Ed was just a psychopath."

"Or, a sociopath who made a very good decision very quickly."

"What the hell is the difference?"

I shook my head. "Sociopathy and psychopathy are very different things. As far as it matters here, a sociopath can mask their symptoms and, the reason I bring it up, they are very good at climbing corporate ladders."

"Are you saying your boss is a sociopath?"

"Have you met him? I think there's a very compelling case for that," I said, gesturing at the corpse he had made.

"But, we don't actually know. Like, maybe the copy just escaped and left us behind."

"The copies aren't trying to escape." I checked the body's pulse just to be sure. There was no heartbeat, but the body was still warm. Definitely not human. Rigor mortis hadn't set in either, and lifting an arm made fresh blood ooze out of the wound. It wasn't congealing. The body was as fake as a special effects prop.

I took a breath and admitted to myself that Ed had been right. The correct thing to do was to kill my clone the instant I saw it. I had to act without thinking and smash its head in before anyone could stop me. Before that though, I had another problem.

"Lucy, can I see your head again?"

"Sure." She wasn't bleeding.

"Would you mind laying down on the table for a moment? I think I can prove that you're actually alive," I lied.

She frowned. "Don't we need to be finding the others?"

"The others will have to eventually come back through here. The door out is at the bottom of the lobby. Wherever they are right now, they're in a dead end and will eventually come back. Better to wait here than miss them in a loop or something. Come on, just lay down. You made me promise I wouldn't abandon you, right? I'm not going to abandon you now."

Willing to please me, Lucy sat down on the table. There should have been a printer, a copier, a fax machine or something there, but the table itself had survived the world's technological regression with no purpose. She vanished below the cubicle wall as I stepped around. There were no computers, but there were landlines, and landlines meant cables. "How do you feel?" I asked, and yanked the phone cable out the back, then ripped it from the ground.

"I don't know, the same? You're not going to do some

weird procedure to me, are you? Gonna jab me with a needle when I'm not looking?"

Wire in hand, I stepped back around and crouched behind her. I could see blood staining her hair again. "Slide back and hang your head off the edge," I said.

She complied, rolling her head back to look at me. The moment the wound became the lowest point on her body, blood started draining out of it again and I stopped taking chances. I looped the wire around her throat. Before she could get a finger under it, I cinched and squeezed. Unable to scream, she kicked her feet and tried to roll. I yanked her off the table and dragged her by the improvised garrot. She hit the floor hard and started clawing at my arms. Her nails raked ragged lines through my flesh as she started to gag and fail to cough.

I could feel the wire stretching in my grasp, the way the rubber dug into my fingers. The only thing I could do was haul her up—make her body weight hang against it and crush her windpipe.

There was something I hadn't accounted for however. I really should have because it was the entire premise of why I attacked her. If she didn't have actual blood flow, there was no blood flow to cut off. Pinching off the arteries could cause loss of consciousness in seconds. Cutting off airflow took minutes. I was basically choking a zombie.

One with nails she used to gouge my eye.

She ripped open my eyelid and almost slashed my cornea. Felt like she might have. I screamed and lost my grip. She elbowed me in a wild thrash, knocking me back. She didn't try to make excuses. She knew the game was up and bolted for the Negotiator. I had put it down to get the wire and she hefted it up with both hands. I was blind in one eye but still managed to grab one of her arms and stop her swing. She grunted. I kicked her in the gut and knocked her into the desk. The Negotiator fell to the floor.

I picked it up.

She made it easy on me, she lunged forward. I swung faster and caught her in the cheek with the head of the wrench. The metal jaw punched through bone and snapped her neck. Her body thumped to the floor, one arm still stretched towards me. She didn't move. She didn't bleed.

I stood over her, breathing hard and feeling the trickle of blood down my face. When my heart rate began to come down, I glanced about until I found a box of tissues. With no better idea, I pulled a wad out and jammed them to the wound. Nothing I could do for the arm cuts, but they'd have to clot on their own.

And then it was just me and my own breathing, standing over the lookalike corpse of a coworker I had promised to protect. I told myself it had been the right thing to do. I even told myself again that she was obviously the clone, but a niggling little thought kept worming in the back of my mind: What if even the real ones had these fake bodies? Did I know I would bleed normally? That I wasn't in a dream logic body?

The clock hand didn't strike three, so I told myself that meant the real Lucy was still alive. She'd probably been the one to brain this Lucy in the stairwell. Lucy was a ladder climber just like Ed. She might have it in her to take decisive action. So I did the only rational thing after that, and started checking her pockets for her ID badge. Her pants had no wallet, and I only then remembered that she had a purse originally. One which I had dumped. I couldn't remember an ID badge in that pile, so I checked her socks, her shoes, and so on.

I had just tugged her shirt up to make sure it wasn't hiding beneath her bra strap when I heard the footsteps. They were heavy, purposeful, and headed towards me. I stood up, grabbing the Negotiator, but they had already seen me. Mikhaila screamed. Shocked, words choked in her throat. She seemed torn between running forward and falling backwards. A strong hand took her by the shoulder, keeping her right in place as she trembled. Chuck strode past her, taking in the carnage. He wasn't the one who had supported her though. That was the other me. The figment of regret, or the alien construct, or the whatever.

The thing that had my badge out of the building narrowed his eyes at me.

"Good news!" I said, and scraped my eyelid off with the tissues. That tore the wound back open and blood once again dribbled into my bleary eye. "I figured out how to tell who's a copy and who's not."

Chuck stepped forward and ran his tongue across his teeth like an old western sheriff. "Oh? And how do you do that?"

I hefted the Negotiator onto my shoulder and gestured around the suite. "It was Ed that gave me the idea. Or, the proof rather. That whole chat with the two Mikhailas? You're not ever going to be able to talk your way out of knowing who is who. You just can't do it. Maybe if we were family members or dating or something, maybe then you'd know the person well enough to know what they would do and say, but not us. We're no better than strangers."

Mikhaila flinched back, hand to her chest. I winced at the sight, but I didn't take my words back. The last thing I wanted was Chuck cutting me open like he had cut Builder. My clone seemed to understand the situation as well, using the two of them like human shields as he watched.

"So, what's the idea? What do you have to prove that you're you? And that you didn't kill the other Mikhaila just like you killed Lucy?"

"Well, I didn't do that. I wasn't able to test her. Why don't the two of you come on over here. Let's all keep a nice, healthy distance and you can tell me what you don't see." I led them over to the corpse Ed had made and stood opposite it.

My clone hadn't taken his eyes off of the Negotiator. "Why don't you give that to Mikhaila?" he asked.

I couldn't jump him. He was too far away, and Chuck stayed between us. So much for my earlier plan. "No," I said, and pointed at the body. "Check it, no rigor mortis and we've been here for hours. It should have set in by now. That's not a human body."

Chuck glanced at Mikhaila, then knelt down and found the same thing I had. "If you're about to tell me the way to check is to kill them and wait four hours..."

"It's not," I said. "It's the bleeding. The clones are... sort of like, I don't know, flesh simulacrum?"

Mikhaila asked, "What the hell is a simulacrum?"

"A simulated recreation of a thing," my simulacra said, taking the words out of my mouth.

"They don't bleed, either."

Mikhaila's eyes went wide. "Lucy bled! You're the one who bandaged her!" she shouted, pointing back at the corpse. "You've gone… no, you are insane. I knew from the moment you trusted my clone instead of me."

I gritted my teeth as she stepped away, shrinking back to stand next to my simulacra. The damn bastard smirked at me. I said, "Lucy was oozing, not bleeding. A real headwound should have bled through that shoddy bandage in an hour or something. But there is no blood pressure in these things. You have to tilt them over to drain them. Look, here," I said as I pulled out Mikhaila's badge. I tossed it to her. "The other admitted she was fake. See? I got it back for you."

Her jaw dropped when she caught it and saw her picture on the card.

"If that's true about the blood," Chuck said, standing up again. He squinted at me. "Then you should have found Lucy's badge. So, where is it?"

"Well… I haven't found that one yet. I didn't have very long. Not like a video game where I just press the loot button, you know?"

My doppelganger cocked his head at me. "Your eye isn't bleeding anymore. Not even oozing."

"What?" I dabbed at it, finding the cut scabbed over, blood crumbling off. "Oh, come on, that's just healing. That was a shallow cut and eyes heal fast."

Chuck pointed his weapon at me. "I'm going to have to ask you to drop the wrench."

I snarled at him. "Listen to me! Cut his head and see if he bleeds! He's the fake."

My simulacra scoffed. "I'm not going to let you cut me based off your bullshit. You're just a murderer."

Had I been alone with him, or even with Mikhaila too, I would have taken my chances. Unfortunately, life was not like in the movies and one good cut could kill me before I escaped. A five pound wrench was not something I could protect myself against a blade with, even one that wasn't particularly sharp.

I did have one advantage though, I knew where the exit was and they didn't. So I ran.

My escape hit a snag when I found the bottom of the lobby flooded. One of the security doors, maybe the one I had smashed, had blown open. I could still reach the elevator door, but I could also reach the stairs to the lower floor. They wouldn't exactly be easy to walk up now that they were vertical–the steps essentially had an angle to them–but I could. The doors that should have led to the parking garage were well out of reach though.

"Fuck." I couldn't see in the water. There wasn't enough light from the overhead windows. I pulled my phone out and tried to power it on. My swim earlier had bricked it though. I had no way of knowing if Builder was lurking behind that door.

I heard my simulacra shout, "He's got my badge! Corner him, capture him!"

I snarled and spun around. The server room was half-illuminated still by the lingering batteries of the processors. It was a crossroads in the office labyrinth, with two other options for me to go. I yanked open one of the other doors and almost dove through before I realized it was a storage closet. This time not for cleaning supplies, but excess filing cabinets. The old things had been packed together, squeezing the room for all its space and provided almost nowhere to hide; nowhere to get the jump on someone.

It was so small that I was able to see the half-form of a human sticking out from the edge of the last cabinet. The toe of their shoe was exposed, and I immediately recognized the narrow tip and slope of the heel. "Lucy?"

"Fuck," she said, jerking her foot back out of sight.

A dozen thoughts raced through my head and none of them made it out my mouth because I heard Chuck running up behind me. Quick with a blade he might have been, but fleet of foot he was not. I glanced back; one other door that could go anywhere and no time to check. I jumped into the closet, shut the door, and groped in the darkness for the handles of the filing cabinets. I pulled them out as quietly as I could, praying the plastic rollers wouldn't screech as I used them to barricade the door.

Not the grandest form of defense, but maybe it would do.

"Don't move," Lucy said.

"Shut up," I whispered back. I didn't turn my head, but I did put a finger to my lips and point at the door.

Thankfully, she shut up. Chuck reached the server room. I saw the sweep of his cell phone light pass through the door frame, right over it. I heard his steps, the way he bumped into the toppled server racks. Step by step, I tracked him across the room and to the lobby. Then someone else joined him, heavy footsteps–too heavy to be Mikhaila. "Think he crossed over?" Chuck asked.

"That implies the exit really is over there."

"Not sure why a clone would lie about that. Seems like great bait, don't you think?"

"Maybe, but if he had gone in the water, wouldn't we see a wet spot over there?"

"He could have gone through that door down there, or maybe he took the stairs?"

I wanted to scream. If the other door had led to the emergency stairs, and I had gotten stuck in a closet, that was just my luck. Then I heard my simulacra say, "I don't think he took the stairs. I'd hear the echoing." Fair enough logic there.

"And we're sure he came this way?" Chuck asked.

"You saw as well as I did."

"He wouldn't be stupid enough to hide in a closet, would he?"

"Seems like it's that, or he did dive in."

"Check the door," Chuck ordered, and my blood went cold.

"Me? You do it."

"He's your clone, ain't he?"

"You have a weapon!"

"Yeah, which is why I'll come in and save you. This is a long blade, not a dagger. I need room to swing."

"Oh come on, what are you? A kendo guy?"

"Just do it. He's your clone. He has your badge. I can leave him in there and get out just fine. That means you have to do it."

I swallowed and edged back from the door. I tightened my grip on the wrench and tried to keep my breathing under control. Then I felt something metal poke me in the back.

"I said don't move," Lucy hissed, pressing the knife against my back.

That steadied my breathing, set it right to zero. While I was trying to figure out what to say to Lucy, I heard my simulacra groan and walk over. Lucy caught her own breath as the door handle rattled, and then it banged into the filing cabinet. "What the?" he said. "Oh son of a bitch, he is in here."

"Well? Get it open."

My simulacra shoved again, knocking the cabinet into the next one and not budging the door. Then he kicked it hard. The whole thing rattled and papers rustled, but nothing moved. "I can't. What the hell is blocking it?"

"Filing cabinets," Chuck said. "Maybe one rolled loose. Try jiggling it, it might just be a little snag."

My simulacra rattled it, but that did nothing. He kicked again. "You got a battering ram or something?"

"We might be able to find a fire ax."

"Well, I'd fucking like to have one of those anyway. Where?"

"If I knew where one was, do you think I'd be using a griddle blade? I just figure that one of the security offices probably has one. They've probably got guns too."

"So, what? We stay here with him trapped in a closet, if he is in there, and send Mikhaila to find a tool?"

I was so screwed it wasn't even funny, but Chuck saved me. "We could do that, on the assumption he is in there… or, we give something else a try. If the exit is over there, we can get someone out."

"With whose badge? Mikhaila's?"

"That's an option, but well, we don't really know that she's the real one, now do we? I've got a safer plan. Let's get you out of here."

"How? He has my badge in there."

"Maybe we don't need your badge."

"I'm not using Mikhaila's."

"Not hers either," Chuck said. "There's another option. While I was exploring earlier, I came down here, to the lobby specifically. Did some climbing around and I got lucky. I found Seamus' ID badge. Let's go find the exit and see if that works. Probably won't, but maybe it will. If you get out, well, there'll be no debating identity after that, now will there? Mikhaila and I can just deal with your clone, I get his badge, she has hers, we all leave."

"I don't know if that will work. ID badges are specific to the individual–"

"I'm sorry, I wasn't asking. That's my fault. I'm telling you that's what you're going to do. Understood? Because if you don't, I'll cut you down and side with the one in the closet."

Nobody spoke after that. We all breathed shallowly, quietly. I heard footsteps crossing the room. One splash in the water. A second. More footsteps in the server room. I heard Mikhaila say, "Ryan, if you are in there, and if you're the real one… I'm really sorry I never apologized sooner."

I didn't know what to say to that, and before I could think of something, I heard a third body splash into the water. "I think they're gone… unless the other Mikhaila shows up."

Lucy's hand started to shake. "What the fuck is going on?"

I didn't know how to answer that without using a question, so I just asked, "Did you see another version of you running around?"

"Yes! And everything's wrong. I'm in some kind of

nightmare world and these stupid girls keep saying I should go play nice with everyone, then laugh at me!"

That explained a lot. "Do you believe in magic?"

"You had better not say you're a wizard or something."

"I'm not, but I think those teenagers are witches. They've pretty much said so. Could you put the knife down though?"

"How can I trust you?"

"You're gunna have to make that decision for yourself. There's nothing I can say that will convince you. Just what other people are doing and saying…"

She pulled the knife off of me, and I was able to turn around. She had a chef knife, plenty lethal. The fact she hadn't stabbed me already made me sigh with relief. "What the hell is going on, Ryan?"

"I only know some things. Do you have your ID badge?"

"No, it was missing when I woke up. Someone stole it from me."

I arched an eyebrow at her. She looked just like the simulacra I killed, but no headwound. "Did you see yourself? Walking around and talking to people like she was you?"

"I did, yeah. And I've seen two Mikhailas, and by the sound of it, two Ryans."

I nodded. "Each of us has a clone. The clone has our badge. We need to get that badge and find the door out, and badge out to escape. Apparently, that's the rules of the world."

"Oh yeah?" she asked. "How do you know that?"

"Do you remember when the building got re-scrambled?"

"Yeah."

"That was because Ed badged out."

"Okay, so how do I know you're the real Ryan?"

"As opposed to a simulacrum made the moment we entered this fucked up world?"

"Yeah."

"There's a couple giveaways. First, they have the badges out. Not super reliable since they can hide them, but maybe. Second, they bleed wrong. More like a Hollywood prop than a person. Third, if you convince them you've confirmed they're a clone, they drop the pretenses. All that said, why don't you stop worrying about whether I'm real and concern yourself with whether I can help you?"

She picked the knife up and sneered at me. We barely had any light at all, and I could still see the set of her body as she looked down at me. "Oh? And what the hell can you do for me?"

"Wow, you really are different from your clone. Stress really changes you, doesn't it?"

"Don't compare me to some lookalike."

I sighed. "You know what, you can either trust me and have an ally, or I'll leave. Do you really want to be alone in the dark again?" We stared at each other. It didn't take much light to hold one another's gazes. I sagged a bit and asked, "You've been hiding alone in the dark, haven't you?"

"Maybe."

"So, your phone still has charge?"

"Yes."

"Come on, give me a light, would you?" After my un-planned nap in the bathroom, my phone was hanging on at eight percent. I didn't dare wake it up.

She turned her phone's light on, and kept her knife be-tween me and her as I closed the shelves. Eventually, I opened the door and stepped through. "Come on," I said. "I already killed your clone. Let's find your badge and get you out of here, alright?" I may not have made my promise to the real Lucy, but I had still given my word. I meant something to protect her, to get her out of this fucked up world. I was going to do it, and I was going to get myself out. Failure wasn't an option.

She hesitantly reached out and took my hand, a delicate and almost romantic gesture amid the blinking LEDs like disco lights. She put her trust in me and I pulled her out of the darkness. It felt good to hold her hand.

Then the world shuddered.

4

3:57

The image in front of me warped. The colors blurred together and I had to blink a few times to resolve them in my brain once more. Lucy wasn't standing in front of me anymore. The door from the server room now led to the cafeteria. But, that wasn't to say she was completely missing. I rationally understood what had happened, of course.

Someone had used Seamus' ID badge. They had escaped the building. Whenever someone successfully badged out, the rooms were reset. The deck of cards was reshuffled and re-dealt. Every door connected somewhere else and the connections were done by magic. Nobody was out there lining one room up to the next. Just like that mop handle I found, sliced in half, the world jumped to the conclusion, and cut through the problems.

When Chuck made my simulacra use Seamus' badge, the building scrambled connections once again, to hide the exit from us. And Lucy had been standing with arm outstretched to me at the time.

I found myself holding her limp and bleeding hand, severed at the elbow. I could hear her screams of agony echo, matching my own screams of panic.

Once again, the rooms had shuffled. I was alone in the dark, clutching Lucy's severed arm to my side. I had it wrapped in my shirt to keep it clean. Maybe it could be reattached. I'd heard once that the issue with reattaching limbs was how ragged the cut was. I couldn't imagine a cleaner cut than what the door had done to her. Rot could do it too though. I didn't have ice to put it on.

There was nothing else I could do. I was lucky I was level headed enough to think that through at all.

Luckily, I was standing next to the new exit. One of the four doors in the server room was the way out, but I didn't have a badge to escape. I had never found the one on Lucy's copy and my own copy was probably the one that had just gotten out. I wondered if that meant I was trapped permanently, but that path led to despair so I put it out of mind.

It felt like the girls had put it there to taunt me.

"Sucks, doesn't it?"

I spun to see the unnamed witch behind me. The door behind her was open to my cubicle suite. She shrugged her slender shoulders at me. "Sorry about that. You can blame Tanya for it."

"For this?" I asked, holding up Lucy's arm like it was just some inanimate thing.

She shuddered and pulled back. "I meant the exit. That...

wasn't supposed to happen. You know, you people are very violent."

I felt something inside me fade. Some essence of civility, of restraint. It left me and in its wake I was furious. "What the fuck do you expect us to do? You haven't even told us your name."

She sighed and turned up her hands. "My name's Bella. And for what it's worth, I blame Ed. He set the tone all wrong. Chuck too, faking his death and all that."

"You people trapped us in here with a monster! And clones! And fuck knows what else!"

Bella put a hand on her hip and arched an eyebrow at me. "Okay, first off. Builder isn't a monster. That's very rude. Second of all, you're trapped in here with yourselves. Don't you think you need to look in a mirror if your instinct is to kill yourself?"

A sadist magical girl wannabe, who had us trapped in a nightmare fighting each other to the death, was lecturing me. Then I remembered what Lucy's clone had proposed, a way to break the spell.

I clubbed her with the Negotiator. I didn't think about it, I just did it. My mind was too worn out and I was holding a severed arm and I had just killed somebody and I cracked her skull open.

For a moment, I stood over her panting. My chest was tight. I couldn't breathe and I couldn't believe what I had done. I had to wipe some sweat from my eyes as I felt vomit roll up my stomach. When I blinked my eyes open though, the body was gone. It had been there, and then it wasn't, like I had hallucinated the whole thing.

Maybe this entire world was a hallucination.

"Well that was rather rude." The voice was Bella's, without a doubt, but the tone had changed. The enunciation had cleaned up slightly. The mere hint of a deeper register. When I spotted her, standing to my side, her body matched the voice; mature. No longer barely a teenager, she had the body of a twenty-year old college student. The tank top was the same, but now it clung to her new curves. I wasn't looking down at her anymore.

"What the hell?" A poet I was not.

"I thought you were the smart one?"

"What gave you that idea?"

"Well, you did find a flaw in the spell."

"So, I was right? That was the fake Lucy?" There had been the chance that all of us had fake bodies.

"Yes, you can rest easy about that, even if Bella would love to twist your head on backwards just to watch you trip."

"So…?" I gestured at her and part of me wondered whether I should attack her again. It had achieved something. "What's this then? More magic?"

"I would suggest that you don't spend your time worrying about it, alright? The spells holding this world together just became entangled," Bella said, gesturing to me and then the exit.

"So, you are magical girls."

She sighed and pinched between her eyebrows. "I'm clearly expecting too much. I shouldn't care. I should be like Tanya. I know I should and yet here I am. You'd think I'd have learned by now, but you mortals always surprise me."

I held out my arms and bared my chest. "What the hell do you expect from me? Nothing got explained!"

She sighed and when she looked at me again, her face was set in a professional mask. "The figments are not supposed to leave this world. There's nothing to them that can leave. Okay? So when Chuck forced your figment to badge out he destroyed one of the badges for nothing. You do realize what that means, right?"

"What? That one of us can't get out?"

"Exactly. A whole lot of magic nothing just set sail in the lifeboat named Seamus."

"But… we have an extra badge somewhere, right?"

Bella paused, hand mid gesture as part of her lecture. Her brow furrowed. "Ryan, what the hell are you talking about?"

I shrugged. "Seamus died. His figment is somewhere around here, we get that badge, that's enough for everyone. Chuck isn't evil. He must have realized that too and figured it was safest to just use two badges and get me and my figment out. Right?" The two of us stared at one another. Except, that didn't add up. Wasn't it Seamus' badge my clone had just used? Then where was Chuck's? Silence grew thick and heavy as she waited for me to say more but all I could say was a weak, "Right?"

"You didn't figure that out by now?"

The knot in my throat was worse than the day I had asked Mikhaila out. That clawing grip of doubt and fear. Enough apprehension to choke. "Figure what out?"

"Seamus is Chuck. Chuck is Seamus. The body you saw? That was his figment, not him. He already has his own badge.

Ryan, this isn't his first time in this world. He knows what he's doing."

The knot of fear swallowed my mind. The anger, the frustration, I lost track of it completely as I started thinking over everything that had happened. From the start, I should have realized that I was the last to wake up. I still had no idea why that was, but obviously things had happened before I had woken up. Mikhaila had left the cubicle suite–I had never asked her why she left me behind instead of trying to wake me up. Lucy had encountered her clone. Seamus had been killed and, I guess, left to be found by Builder. If Chuck had killed his own clone, like Ed did, then Builder really wasn't a monster. It had just been there. The fact that it didn't chase Mikhaila and I into the HR suite suddenly made sense.

Then I remembered what Tanya had said when she saw Chuck; "How completely not nice to see you again, Chuck."

I realized the answer to one of our earlier problems. We hadn't known what would happen if the wrong person used the badge to leave. Now, I did. The badges were like tickets out. You left as the person you badged out as; your mind, their body. He must have given Seamus'... his own badge to my clone. Seamus' body was overweight, unpleasant, and old. It also wasn't his original body, so he would have no attachment to keeping it. Shoving me into it and taking my body would be far better for him.

Hell, it was almost a recipe to eternal youth, in a vampiric body-snatching sort of way.

I knew I was grasping and had no concrete proof, but all the pieces of the puzzle fit. The only people who could confirm my hypothesis were the girls, the game masters as he had called them. At some point in my shock, I had sat down with my back to the exit.

I really wanted to throw up, but there was nothing in my stomach to puke. I wasn't bleeding from my face anymore either so I sat there wondering if all of us were in fake bodies.

What was I to do? The repeating question that just kept looping back around to me. I wondered if the hours had finally accumulated to the point of days. I wanted to go check if the clocks said three minutes to four now, but I couldn't leave.

I sat with my back to the exit and waited, tapping the Negotiator against a metal rack like a chime. Again and again I rang the bell to let everyone know where I was. If Chuck wanted to leave with my body, he'd damn well have to go through me to do it. What was more, Lucy needed to get to a hospital and I hoped she would come to the sound.

I had no choice but to wait, but I at least waited aggressively.

Unfortunately, the first person to show up was Tanya. She just casually took a seat in a corner beside Bella, atop one of the server racks that Builder had ruined. She crossed her legs and planted her chin in her hand with a grin. "Don't mind me. I won't say a word, promise. I'm just here for the show, you know? This is better than television!"

"What happens if I kill you? Do you get older too?"

Her grin vanished. "Wouldn't you like to know?"

"I think I'd be justified. It's self-defense, isn't it?"

"As if you're going to escape here."

"Careful," I said, smirking back at her. "If I do get stuck

in here, I'd be stuck with you. You don't want to be enemies with your new roommate, do you?"

She stuck her tongue out at me, then both of us heard the approaching footsteps. Her grin came back as Chuck strolled in from the cubicle suite and looked down at me.

I gave him my attention and said, "How very not nice to see you again, Seamus. Still got all the badges?"

Chuck/Seamus/Whoever frowned and glanced around the room. The haze of light behind me was dim, just a little sliver of window along one side of the door, but enough to know the exit was to my back. He also saw Tanya and sneered at her. His eyes glowed red in the glow of dying servers. "You must be the real one then."

"Wasn't that obvious?" I asked, waving the wrench in the air before me.

Chuck scratched his chin and nodded his head, side eying Tanya again. "It was likely, yes. I guess the cat's out of the bag then. Which one squealed? I figured Tanya was enjoying the chaos too much to tell."

She giggled and pointed a thumb at Bella.

"So this isn't your first time in this world?" I asked, pushing myself up to my feet, one eye on the oversized kitchen utensil.

Chuck smiled and shook his head. "Sorry, kid. I'm not really here to chat. Tell you what though. I don't feel like fighting you and I hope you don't feel like fighting me. I wanted to just slip out and be done with this but someone had their finger on the scale, they nudged the odds, they put you in my way. At the end of the day, I'd rather play it safe, you know what I mean?"

"You were going to kill me," I said, staring into his smoldering eyes. "Where's Mikhaila?"

He scoffed. "I don't know, somewhere back there. She heard Lucy screaming and went looking. That was nice of her, don't you think?"

"If you did something to her, I will make you regret it."

"Gunna kill me like you killed Lucy?"

"That was her clone."

"You sure about that? This is my second time and even I wasn't sure you were you and I've known you for the last three years, Ryan. You're not exactly a hard guy to read."

"So you are Seamus."

"Was," he said, laughing down his nose at me. "Oh man, you have no idea how good it is to have my voice back. Like, don't get me wrong, I played it up for sure. Nobody is willing to hound you about deadlines if you can just call up HR for discrimination like that. But damn, it's going to be good to trade up. Or, well, down in terms of age."

I felt the tightness in my chest again–the fear and anxiety. "These aren't our bodies, are they?"

He shook his head and pulled out an ID badge from his pocket. In the gloom, I couldn't tell whose it was. "No, these are our bodies. If it makes you feel better, you're still you. The metaphysics are a bit complicated. I was never one for theology. But here, we can make peace."

"Because of you there aren't enough."

"Yeah, someone has to lose now. If you had been the clone though, everything would have been nice and tidy."

"I would have been stuck in your body. Isn't that right?"

"Wasn't mine in the first place," Chuck said.

Tanya snickered. "Well," she said, "You know what they say, ownership is four fifths of the law?"

I squeezed the grip of the wrench. "Who'd you kill? Last time? No, not who. How many did you kill to save yourself, Chuck?"

"Me? I didn't kill anybody"

Tanya laughed.

"Liar," I said.

"Murder is a legal thing, Ryan. Don't you understand? When we get out of here there's not going to be any evidence. Even your memory will be disregarded. It will be like this never happened. As far as anyone else is concerned, I didn't kill anybody. But, I'll tell you what. I said this a moment ago. I don't want to fight you, Ryan. I'll cut you a deal."

I unclenched my teeth. My body trembled. "Does that deal involve you giving me all the badges and fucking off?"

His smirk broadened. "Not quite. What's that though?" He pointed to the bloody bundle of cloth that contained Lucy's arm. "I think I can take a guess. I heard the screaming too. Is that what I think it is?"

"That's none of your business."

He laughed. "That's something, ain't it? Let me guess, her foot? Did her foot get cut off when your clone badged out?"

"No."

"Her arm then," he said, and I must have reacted. "She lost her arm, oh how tragic. You know, that can't be put back, don't you? These bodies aren't our bodies, they're constructs of our minds. You see? If she lost her arm like that, even if she were to leave she'd never have feeling in it again."

I pivoted my gaze to Tanya. "Is that true?"

"Yeah, pretty much," she said. "This is just like that movie *Simulations and Simulacra*. You die in the map and you die in the desert of the real. The body can't survive without the mind."

Her reference went over my head. "What are you trying to get at Chuck? For someone who didn't come here to chat, you're sure running your mouth." I wasn't completely certain I could take him in a fight. I really didn't know which of us was more fit, or more experienced for that matter. The footing sucked, a massive tangle of cables and shadows—maybe that was why Chuck had rethought fighting me.

"How about I give you your badge? And you fuck off right now, save your own skin."

I narrowed my eyes. "Why would you do that?"

He shrugged. "I'll take Lucy's body. Doesn't have to be yours, you know. She's got the best career prospects of any of us too. I'd prefer a male body of course, but I'm a reasonable guy. I'll take a safe escape. Besides, like we just established, she wouldn't be able to use her own body anymore. Not properly."

"So you'd be killing her instead of killing me?"

"Someone's gotta die, kid. One way or another, it ain't gunna be me."

I wondered if that line might have worked better on someone else; someone who didn't work with deaths on a daily basis. I had lost track of the amount of people who had unloaded on me about how unfair it was their spouse or child's killer was let off the hook for so-called self-defense and then casually mentioned the armed robbery, or the mugging, or the car jacking. We were actually trained to check for that kind of thing because life insurance doesn't pay out in those circumstances. That made me very familiar with what qualified as killing in self-defense or defense of another.

That gave me just enough mental strength that I stepped forward and whipped the wrench at him as hard as I could.

Chuck shrieked, twisting away. The head slammed into his side with a crunch. I heard him wheeze in shock. Pain must have paralyzed him because he couldn't even take a swing at me as I dove forward. My shoulder hit him in the hips and both of us went down. We landed on the mess of cables, groping at one another in the darkness. I grabbed handfuls of pants and got a finger in his belt. Something hard slammed into my skull as I hooked a finger into his belt. His breath was a wet rasp. Coughs burst from him between every movement. I tried to climb atop him and slam my elbow into his side. Whatever I hit crunched like cardboard.

Then his shoe caught me in the gut, hard. In the moment of recoil, he planted his shoe onto my chest and shoved me off. A jagged edge of metal–broken rack–ripped through my side. Chuck shouted, "Fuck! Where?" He was on all fours, groping across the floor for a glint of white. He grabbed at his pockets and found them empty too.

I did nearly the same, but I wasn't looking for the badge. Every movement burned. My muscles spasmed and twitched like they were tearing themselves apart. I could feel the blood running down my side and wondered what would happen if that were to run out. But I found what I was looking for and wrapped my fingers around the handle of the Negotiator again.

"Looking for this?" Mikhaila asked, and I knew it was the

clone. I could see it in her posture and hear it in her tone. She held the badge Chuck had dropped.

"Give it here," Chuck demanded, rising up with his weapon pointed towards her.

I slumped back, hitting the exit as I squeezed the cut across my side. "You better stop her," I said, trying to keep the smirk off my face. "If she gets away, how are you ever going to find her?" I really needed to get the smirk off my face. If he didn't get her, I'd have to get her. She probably had my badge.

"If you make me chase you," he said as he straightened his back and stood like I hadn't broken his ribs. "You will regret it."

"You won't get the chance," she said, backpedaling into the hall she had come from.

Chuck frantically glanced about himself once more. He even pulled out his phone and flipped on the flashlight, but no second badge appeared. He snarled at me and stomped after Mikhaila's clone.

"Aren't you going too? Or are you just going to leave?" Tanya asked.

I worked my tongue around my mouth, felt blood on my lips. A prod at my skull found a split in my hairline. Chuck must have been hitting me with the base of the gridle blade. The flow had already stopped though, and I was adjusting to the pain. "I'm going." I picked up Lucy's arm.

"You sure?" Tanya asked as Chuck started running after Mikhaila. "That was a pretty slick move. Now's your chance."

There was a bit of light coming in from the exit, enough that I could see what I had stolen from Chuck's pocket. I had

Lucy's badge. Not as good as my own, but it was something. "Yeah, I'm sure," I said, and chased after the two of them.

I had never really been in a stand up fight before, especially not while sober. A pair of drunken brawls in college hardly counted and certainly didn't prepare me for something that felt like a duel–like the two of us were gunslingers in the old west. It wasn't high noon though, there was no sun in the sky and the clocks said it was three minutes to four.

I could barely remember the way back to the exit, but that didn't matter. I would have all the time in the world, soon enough. Chuck had chased the clone Mikhaila and I had chased him. All three of us had ended up on the gravel rooftop outside our suite, the one where I had confirmed she was the fake. It extended out into the mist and above the water like a bridge to nowhere, a deadend she had entered by choice.

I was breathing hard and so was he. Both of us were bruised and bleeding and that gave me time as I limped after them across the soaked gravel to think about how ridiculous we all looked. We weren't fighters. We weren't thugs or criminals or fantasy heroes. We were as ordinary as the things we had for weapons. The girls must have been loving our little show.

"Give it here," Chuck ordered. He was walking better than I could. The damage was all in his chest. I could see by the way his shoulders were slumped to one side, that one arm was locked up.

"I will do nothing of the sort," the fake Mikhaila said. She held the ID card up in the air and smirked. "You can't catch up to me, but he can catch up to you."

Chuck glared over his shoulder at me, but turned back to her. "You're not even real. You're a fake. A ghost!"

I snarled and started after him, picking the Negotiator back up. "You're the ghost, Chuck. You killed somebody to survive last time, right? That's what you said. That means you should be dead. You were in someone else's body like a parasite and you were going to do it again. You're nothing but a ghost possessing someone else."

"Shut up! I survived. I fucking lived my live in that festering carcass of fat and disgust. You think I would have chosen to be like that?"

Mikhaila laughed and jumped up on one of the sky lights. She towered over us, teetering as she strolled the edge. "Does that somehow give you the right to kill someone else? Because you had it hard? Everyone here has had it hard. They're going to have it hard. Everything about life sucks. Haven't you figured that out? Nobody is going to cry for you, you murderer."

"Oh, shut up. You're nothing but a memory," Chuck said, and he looked at me once more. There was a softening in his expression. I couldn't see the hunched tension in his shoulders anymore. He sneered at Mikhaila. "You're a little figment the witches plucked from our brains. You're cruel because you're a memory of pain. Your job is to bog us down and keep us from leaving because that's what you are. If you were really set on keeping us here–you know, this is the silly part, Ryan–if you were really set on it, you would never have shown up. You'd have taken the card and vanished, but you can't do that. It's impossible for you to leave us alone. It's against your nature."

I couldn't read Mikhaila's expression. I had to remind my-self that she wasn't the real one. I swear I saw something like a smirk on her face. It made the hair on the back of my neck stand up as I heard water pour onto the gravel. It splashed and trickled from one edge of the roof. I stumbled back as my eyes picked out the shadow of Builder rising from the water. He climbed up without a noise of his own. I couldn't even hear his breathing.

The killer shrank back, putting Mikhaila between him and it. I saw him try to stretch his body out, to check how he could move and what hurt. I doubted either of us stood a chance against the creature.

Mikhaila laughed and held out her hands to either side. "A regret I may be, but don't you know? Regret can do so much more than keep you stuck in place. A strong enough regret can even kill–"

Builder bit her hand off.

He reached up behind her and snapped his teeth around her hand that held the ID badge. We all heard the crunch of bone as his enormous teeth shredded through her limb. Mikhaila shrieked. Panic punched me in the chest, but I didn't know what to do except watch. She tumbled, swinging her jagged stump through the air. Blood arced as she hit the gravel and screamed.

Chuck screamed too.

I saw him sprint forward, his kitchen blade overhead. He hacked at Builder's face, cutting into the monster's cheek with all his strength.

The creature did bleed. It did have muscles beneath its hide. The noise it made wasn't a whimper of pain, but a growl of irritation. It reared up like an elephant and stomped down on Chuck. The would-be killer didn't leap back in time and I heard the crunch of his ankle.

The blade went sliding away from him and he miserably tried to crawl after it. Builder just turned his back on both of them. He slipped back into the water like a leviathan and left me with both of them.

My fatigue gave me enough time, as I stood watching, to remember a few things. Builder had been human. Somewhere in that misshapen body was, or had been, the mind of a man. If badges were our bodies, he might have finally gotten a ticket out. I couldn't blame him, even if I would have to do something about it.

Mikhaila wasn't shouting anymore. I had to remind myself that it was just a simulacra. A special effects prop that looked just like her—now twisted in agony and clutching the splintered bone of her right arm. The scant amount of blood in her fake body had already spilled out and soaked into the gravel. There wasn't any blood pressure to her skull because it was all spilling out her arm. She gave some grunts, some twists and jerks. Whenever she moved, it pumped more of the blood out of her body and I watched her skin deflate until she stopped entirely.

Chuck was bleeding more. He was grunting and gasping in pain, dragging himself over to his weapon and cursing God.

I put my foot on the handle of his weapon, shoving it down into the gravel as his fingers tried to reach it.

"God fucking damn it," he said, the tremors in his body uncontrollable. "I should have fucking killed him. Should have done it when I had the fucking chance. Shouldn't have left him behind."

I wanted to puke. I couldn't think of any words to say. When I swung the Negotiator down, I didn't even feel the impact.

Tanya showed up while I was digging through the fake Mikhaila's pockets. I wasn't surprised by her approach. Given how quiet the world was, any sound seemed amplified, especially the light crunch of gravel, the padding of tennis shoes. I could tell from the sound that the person didn't weigh a hundred pounds. She moved like a fairy. "What do you want?" I asked.

She stopped around the corner, just close enough that we could see each other. She smiled. "I want to know if you feel bad now that you're a murderer."

I gave up on the fake Mikhaila's pockets. She didn't have another badge. Of course she didn't, the real Mikhaila had her own badge. I had given it to her. I rose and faced the teenage witch. "Not really," I said. "Maybe that will change when I sleep on it. Maybe I'll be tormented by nightmares and will need years of therapy. Maybe I'll have to turn to religion and find salvation in Christ."

She laughed.

"But, right now? I really couldn't care less about him. I guess I'm wondering if I ever liked him at all. I swear I spent more time avoiding him than talking to him this past year. To find out he was a killer? I don't know, I guess it just doesn't really do much for me."

Tanya grinned. She looked like she was auditioning for a horror movie. "That means you're a psychopath. You didn't flinch when you saw the first body, did you? And that was before you know about the figments. And Lucy? Poor dear old Lucy who you tried to strangle? Yeah, you're a psychopath for sure."

"No, I'm not."

"Yeah, you are. A total psycho. You're whacked in the head. A nut! You belong in an asylum. They gotta strap you down and jab you full of lithium. You've killed two people already and who knows how many more will be your victims next. Give you a gun and you'd be going for a high score."

"I'm not a psycho and I know you know that," I said, crouching down to be eye level with her. "You might act like a child, but you're not young, are you? If you live here that means you've been here a long, long time. You've seen people come and go, and we might be nothing more than fleeting entertainment for you and your friends, but you at least understand what humans are like."

Her smile had lost some of the maliciousness. She shifted her weight back as she took in my glare. "Yeah, that's why I'm calling you a psycho, you psycho."

"Sorry, but I'm not going to feel bad about being forced to kill someone, especially scum like that and magic monsters."

"Sounds like something a psychopath would say."

It was my turn to laugh at her. "Stop acting like you can bullshit me."

"Oh yeah?" Tanya asked, planting her hands on her hips. "And what would Mikhaila have to say about this? She'd call you a psycho if she heard you now."

"It doesn't matter. Because she didn't hear me, and she's not going to. She's going to leave this fucking place and not look back," I said as I rose and walked past Tanya. I stopped only to grab Lucy's arm and head back into the maze.

"What?" she shouted at my back. "You're just going to give them the badges? You're going to let them leave and be the martyr? Is that it?"

I glanced over my shoulder. "I'm only a martyr if I die. That's not a given. Maybe I'll stick around and kill you over and over and over again. I bet you won't be very young for very long, now will you?"

"You fucking psycho!"

The way I was grinning at her, I couldn't say she was lying. I just wanted that catharsis though. I wanted to see her smug face shatter. My body and mind were numb. I felt like I was carrying the weight of Chuck and Lucy on my shoulders, and saying I was justified didn't change it. I trudged away from her, back into the office building and back through the long tangle of rooms and doors, stairs and halls.

It took me a while, but I got close enough to hear them talking. Mikhaila and Lucy had found each other and the exit while I was away. I found them sitting against one another, huddled up in the light of the exit door. Lucy seemed non-responsive. Her half of the conversation was grunts and mumbles.

Mikhaila had been saying, "It will be alright. Just hang in there. We'll get you to a hospital."

"Here," I said as I walked in. The bloody bundle passed from me to her, followed by her ID badge. "Take it."

Lucy just stared at the badge. I was just starting to wonder if we would have to force her through the motions when she grabbed the badge. Her grip was feeble and I quickly knelt down to help her up. Mikhaila took most of the weight, being on her uninjured side, but I did what I could. She stumbled over between us, her hand trembling as she looked at the badge scanner.

"I'm sorry," she said, hand half-way to the scanner.

"Don't apologize, just get to a hospital," I said, trying to nudge her forward.

"I spent this whole time hiding," Lucy said, and tears were running down her face. "This whole time. The clones. The fighting. All of it. I didn't do anything. I never do the right thing. God damn it, I'm sorry."

Mikhaila winced and looked over Lucy's head to meet my gaze. "Hey, don't worry about it. You're hurt. Get out of here. Just put your hand down and you'll be gone."

"No, I want to say this now. I'm sorry! I shouldn't even have this fucking job. I fucking lied on my resume. You know, I didn't even graduate college. Can you believe that? They didn't check."

Lucy genuinely seemed like she was about to die. I could feel her body temperature dropping. I looked at Mikhaila, hoping she knew what to say. She had been the one to talk to Morgan but now she seemed lost in her own world. I took a breath. "Call them up after you get your arm reattached or something. Have your breakdown after you get to a doctor."

Lucy sniffled in a line of snot and tears. She nodded more than she had to and mumbled something, then touched her ID badge to the scanner.

She vanished.

5

3:58

One moment I was holding onto her, the next I wasn't. There was a lingering feeling like spiderwebs across my fingers but the only remains of Lucy were her ID badge–now blank. It slid off the scanner and fell to the dark ground. That resolved the whole question about teleportation and faded ID badges.

"I guess she was real," Mikhaila said.

I bent down to get the blank card. "How do you know?"

"When the other you scanned his badge, there was a crack like glass."

I stood up and looked at her, nothing more than a shadow in a dark room. The batteries in the servers were all dying and none of the doors led outside. We didn't even have the glow of our phones anymore. We were like ghosts, and in all likelihood, I was as good as dead.

"Here," I said, and gave her her own badge. "Find the exit

and get out of here. It's just me, you, and the witches now. There's no rush."

I could feel her fingers close around the plastic. "Where's yours?"

"They took it from me," I said. "I'm going to have to get it back."

"Will you be able to?"

"I figure, on a long enough time scale, I'll eventually get it back. Time doesn't move here, remember? All the clocks are stuck and I think we're coming up on two days, but I was never really hungry or thirsty. Come on."

Of the four doors, I picked one at random. Light poured in as soon as I did and I laughed because we were back in the cafeteria. I strolled in, my body feeling heavier than ever, and I sat down next to the window. I peered into the smoke, trying to see if the sculptures were still out there. The girl at the start had said they were, but all I saw was an endless haze.

"Ryan, you're bleeding really bad," Mikhaila said. She wasn't next to me though. She stood almost ten feet away, looking at me.

"We never did find a first aid kit, did we?"

"I can go look again?"

"Sure. If you spot the exit though, just go, alright? I'm going to sit for a bit. I think I'm not actually going to bleed out or anything. Magic, you know? I'll hang in just fine." I put on a smile, but I was worn out.

She saw right through me. "I'll be right back," she said, and started to walk away. I heard her footsteps stop. "Hey, if everyone here had a regret, and that other you was the fake. Was what he said true?"

I felt my body tingle like it wanted to tense up, but didn't have the energy. "I have no idea what my clone said. How the hell could I answer that?"

"You… sorry, he said your issue was college."

Yeah, if it was anything it was that. "That's pretty broad."

"Your dad, he passed away right before you left for college, right? And then you didn't know anyone."

"I didn't make the effort," I said, turning away from her.

"I'm sorry. Everything would have been so different if I had just… been more honest back then."

And then she left. She disappeared from the cafeteria and left me with my memories. Four years that should have been the highlight of my life were spent alone and then I ended up in the working world. I wasn't alone anymore, but it wasn't the earnest embrace of youthful friends. Drinking with coworkers was an exercise in small talk, a playbook of social interactions I had figured out just fine but coworkers didn't open up to one another. People I met online were entirely the opposite. They would open up about anything and everything but would never break anonymity–always at arms length and wholly digital.

Life had passed me by, or rather I had let it flow on without me, and I had no one to share it with.

All three of the girls joined me in the cafeteria. They had gotten their hands on soft drinks and snacks, all of which they dumped on the table between them. They grabbed like seagulls fighting over bread, yanking candy out of one another's grasps.

And they all grinned at me as they did.

"Are you feeling better?" Bella asked. She was on my right,

just as old as I had left her last time, which made her seem more mature than the others. She always had acted more mature though. Maybe my brain was playing tricks on me.

"No."

"Eat," Morgan ordered, practically shoving a chocolate bar in my face.

Tanya laughed. "Waste of food. He's just going to die."

I took the chocolate and ate it. I could barely taste the sweetness, but it went down and warmed my stomach. It felt like a bit of life in me, and my head started to clear. Maybe I just wasn't able to feel the hunger, and my body needed food just the same. Going on two days without food wouldn't kill me, but I couldn't imagine it felt good.

"So, what's the point?" I asked, tossing the wrapper aside.

"The point of what?" Morgan asked.

"This place."

"It's so we have somewhere to live, duh," Tanya said.

"If you just wanted to have guests, I can think of more pleasant ways to invite people. If you were billionaires and wanted the thrill of hunting us down, I've at least seen that movie. I understand the taboo and what you get out of it. But were we really that entertaining to you?"

Bella sighed and set her elbow on the table. "Your mistake is thinking we have any particular control over who comes here. That's what happened, after all, you came here. We didn't bring you here. And we haven't really done anything to stop you from leaving either."

I stared at Tanya. Morgan did too. The lying brat found the ceiling to be utterly fascinating and ignored both of us. "So, there was no point?"

Morgan shrugged. "We only have half the story, Ryan. We've never been to Earth, just these memories. People come and pass. Very few stick around. If there's some will that sent you here they've never explained themselves to us so how could we explain it to you? We'd just be lying."

"And we wouldn't want to do that," Tanya added with a smirk.

"If you'd like," Bella said. "You can tell us about yourself. We're going to have plenty of time, since there's no way you're getting your badge back, and once Mihaila leaves there won't be terribly much holding the world together. Just you and Builder."

"I won't be staying," I said, and took another piece of their candy.

That shocked the three of them. For a moment, all they could do was stare at me as I filled my stomach like it was the day after Halloween. Then they spoke to one another, like I wasn't even there.

"He's going to actually go fight Builder, isn't he?" Morgan said

"He's going to get himself killed," Bella said.

"This is disappointing!" Tanya said.

"And here I thought we'd finally get to play some four player games again… until he… you know," Morgan said.

"He must be stupid enough to think he stands a chance," Bella said.

"He doesn't," Tanya said.

"Ladies," I said, rising from my chair. My stomach felt fat with chocolate and nougat and sugar. It was a kind of gluttony I hadn't experienced since high school, but I also felt like a well-fed marathon runner. Just one more reserve of energy to burn while I still could. "I hope these are my final words to you, because the last thing I would want is to be spared by Builder and trapped here. I hope he has the decency to kill me at least, but I have to go fight for my life. The lot of you were horrible to encounter. You've basically tortured me for going on two days. A lot of trauma could have been avoided by better communication on your parts, but hey, maybe that's the nature of the magic. Who am I to say? I don't abduct random people to make clones out of them. I'm not a mad scientist either, I'm just a regular guy. I hope I never see you again and more than that, I hope someday you get abducted like this and attacked by your own clones. If you'll excuse me, I'm going to go make a monster puke out my ID badge."

I left the cafeteria with one real hope: that Mikhaila would find the exit before I did, and before Builder did. I didn't want to see her again though, not inside this nightmare. When I walked—when I went from door to door, hall to hall—I didn't even keep track of where I was going because I had no plan to backtrack. There was no way to systematically narrow down where Builder was because there was no way to systematically eliminate rooms.

I just walked and opened doors and—when given the option—I went down steps instead of up them. It was a small act to conserve my strength.

I didn't find the exit, but I did find the balcony again. My eyelids were drooping again and I felt crusty with blood. I had switched which hand carried the Negotiator so many times my fingers felt numb. So, I couldn't resist the urge to slump down on the railing. Soon enough I was sitting on the table, arms on the railing, and could feel my breathing slowing down. Like the bathroom all over again, I was about to pass out and only had the strength to question if I was just being an idiot.

Then I saw something in the mist. My hazy, sleep-bleary eyes picked out shadows from the mist and above the water. I only noticed because one of them moved; a lumbering, four legged thing. Then my brain knew how to see what was out there and I saw the other shadows. They were the park sculptures, but I also saw cars. At first it was just the profile of a pickup truck. Then I spotted a semi-truck cab, a convertible, and a dozen other twisted shapes that had to be more cars.

I leapt back up. My heart raced as fatigue flushed out. I could see Builder, it had to be Builder. The dangerous little idea that there was another monster out there got ignored. Merely having a path forward gave me renewed strength as I tried to figure out how to seize it–how to get from here to there.

"The water is deep enough," Bella said. She leaned against the door behind me with her arms crossed.

A quick glance over the edge revealed the pool of endless water that surrounded the office building. "Thanks," I said, and took a deep breath.

"Good luck."

I stepped onto the table and onto the railing. The drop was high, but not lethal–I didn't think. It was like stepping off a cliff. Divers did it all the time. I was pretty sure I had seen diving boards set higher. It was only about three stories. I just had to land with my knees bent and a deep breath.

Rationalizing it didn't make the fear stop building inside me, so I just acted.

I stepped off the side. Weightless for a moment, I plummeted off the side of the building. Fear erupted from my stomach outward, catching up with the choices of my brain. I just started to scream and kick as the wall of water rushed up to slam into me. I sank embraced by the wet and the dark.

Then my feet touched a hard bottom and I kicked off forward. Dragging the wrench with me, I swung my arms and pumped my legs. I shot back to the surface and broke through, gasping in air before I floundered down again. Soon my shoes were scraping the bottom and pushing me along and then I was walking–trudging. I waded as if through a swamp and bit by bit the water receded. The asphalt beneath me sloped up so gently I almost couldn't tell if not for the water clearing off my body. But, I kept my gaze on the shadows and pushed on.

If the office building was our domain, a construct of our memories and lives and frustrations, what I entered must have been Builder's domain.

The light was weaker, like twilight, though I saw no cause for the difference. There was no sun overhead, no moon or stars. I could barely make out the yellow and white paint across the asphalt and the grass ditches were hazy seas into which the park structures had been tossed. None of them were rightside up, like they were a collection of kid's toys tossed by the wayside. Still, I recognized a highway overpass when I saw one.

I found seventeen cars piled up, most slammed into an overturned semi-truck trailer. I could faintly see skid marks along the road, leading up to one wreck or another. Panicked turns had gouged ruts of mud and grass where vehicles had swerved into the ditches and crashed. Everything about it looked like it belonged on the evening news as paramedics ran from vehicle to vehicle with stretchers.

There were no car alarms going off. No headlights glaring in the night. No people either. Every car I passed had its doors ripped off, revealing barren and bloodless interiors. The damage clearly hadn't been done by the impacts. I knew what a crashed car was supposed to look like. The only other source of damage came on four legs–a beast looking for its door out. If we came from our office, he must have come from this crash.

Builder spotted me from atop the overpass. I could hear the crunch of glass beneath his feet as he moved over. He loomed down at me without a sound, just the crunch of steel as he trampled the barrier. Down he came, stepping from the overpass and down to the overturned truck. The cargo trailer crumpled with each step, flatting down until he was leveled with the front end of a pickup truck and then down to a commuter car and then he was even with me.

As he approached, I saw how injured he was. Not just the wounds Chuck and I had already given him–the bruises and cuts–but new rips and tears. Blood streamed out of his forelegs and his mouth oozed blood so dark it looked purple. Broken glass and ripped steel had shredded his feet and limbs, his lips and gums. The whole time it had taken me to get here, he had been tearing the cars apart to no success.

"Is this where your door out should have been?" I asked, searching his ancient face for eyes and not finding them.

Builder nodded.

"I guess I should thank you for not taking my door out, even if you took my badge. Did you really think you'd find a badge reader on a car door though?"

Builder turned his head and looked at a heavy truck. The backdoors had been smashed in, revealing the steel reinforcements but not revealing an exit. It looked like it had been a money courier, an armored truck. There wasn't a badge reader on it though, and the inside was empty.

I sighed. "You're a better man than Chuck and that's probably why you're here and he's not."

The creature hung its head. Then its body rocked, a ripple from toe to shoulder to neck and tongue. It did it again and stuck out its tongue. My badge stuck to the end of it as he lifted his head up defiantly.

I nodded, knowing that only one of us could leave. I didn't charge at him though. "How long have you been here? How long did it take for… this to happen?"

Builder cocked his head and I had to reform the question. "Has it been years?" He nodded. "Decades?" He nodded again. "Centuries?" At last, he shook his head. "Were the girls bad to you?" Builder paused, then shook his head again. "Alright, I guess that's good enough."

For a moment, I felt like some kind of caveman. I was half-dressed, bloody and wet, about to fight a monster with nothing but a club. It was goddamn terrifying, but the fear didn't incapacitate me. It chilled me but left me with the knowledge that I had no choice but to fight. There was no runaway and hide.

When Builder pulled his tongue back in and clamped his

teeth shut, I consoled myself that he at least couldn't recklessly bite me. All I had to do was smash his teeth in.

So I charged.

Builder lowered down, slamming into the ground, as he took on a fighting posture of his own.

I had always kind of wanted to trample over cars. There was some half-thought about the high ground, about tactical advantage, but I enjoyed the feeling of denting a hood beneath my feet and charging up the windshield. I mounted the roof and swung the Negotiator as hard as I could into Builder's shoulder. The flesh absorbed it–wet. I could feel the hide and blubber liquify. Then Builder shouldered into the car and knocked it from under me

I tumbled, hitting the concrete hard, and had to roll out of the way, back to my feet, before he could step on me. Despite his enormous size, he wasn't big enough for me to get under him, nor did I have a spear to pierce through. Hoping his hips didn't work too well, I ran for his backside, striking him in the leathery haunch. It earned me an irritated growl.

Builder's tail whipped into me. His hips didn't work well, that was true, but his tail was a huge mass of muscle like a crocodile's. I had seen what it could do against Chuck earlier. When it hit me, I went flying. Next thing I knew I was skidding across the shoulder, into the dirt, tumbling end over end until I smashed up against one of the steel statues.

Surprisingly, I didn't hurt. The blood vomit I spewed a moment later said I was just in shock. I couldn't inhale, not without spasms across my ribs. My vision started to go faint as I realized my left shoulder was dislocated. My legs didn't seem to be broken, but my shoes were missing. The Negotiator was too.

"Oh."

Builder walked over to me, limping two of his legs where I had hit him and still dripping blood. He seemed to look down at my broken body.

"Fuck, I guess that's what I get, eh? Thought I was an action hero or something and look what it got me."

Builder's response was to settle down and rest, just out of reach from me.

"You think I'm going to bleed out and die? Look, that's nice of you, but you're not exactly the kind of company I'd want on my deathbed. Alone with my own mistakes is more my style. You know what I mean?" I wasn't even sure I was enunciating. My head pounded and I could feel more blood trickling down the back of my neck–definitely concussed.

Builder didn't leave though.

"Wouldn't it be cool?" I asked, digging in my pocket with my good arm. "If I had one last trick to pull out? That'd be a real cool thing to do right now. Like a movie hero. I'd pull out something, like a gun, and stare death in the face with a grin." I pulled my hand out of my empty pocket and pointed a finger gun at him. "It's too bad I think I'm already dead, already killed. And, you know, if I did have a trick, I wouldn't have gone in swinging. I would have just used it, you know? But here I am."

Builder lifted his head and looked away from me, back towards the office building.

"Have fun with my body, I guess. Hope it works out for

you. Maybe try getting a different job, eh? Just don't go after Mikhaila. Because then… I'd have to shoot you–bang."

A gun fired. Light blasted into the twilight as sound hammered my ears. I blinked. Metal ratcheted and Builder reeled. The gun fired again and I saw the muzzle flare. I saw the blood spew out the backside of Builder's head too.

The ground shook as the creature collapsed at my feet.

Mikhaila emerged from the mist, carrying a pistol-grip shotgun, and spotted me. "Ryan!"

"Where the fuck did you get that?" I asked, and frowned at my finger gun.

"I found the security office, you idiot. I went everywhere looking for you! Oh my god, you're going to die. We have to get you out of here. Come on."

"Caref–" I howled as she touched my dislocated arm, and she jumped back. "Just, come here," I begged and held up my right arm. She pulled me to my feet, which I managed to stay on for two breaths. Then I collapsed onto her. "I told you to leave."

"Well, I didn't leave you behind," she said, and helped carry me back.

Bella knelt down next to Builder, a sorrowful look on her face as she put a hand to his wheezing chest. "You'll need this," she said, handing Mikhaila my ID badge. Then she looked back to Builder. "I'm sorry, but it was time. You'll be alright moving on. I'm sure of it."

"She brought me here," Mikhaila whispered as she took my weight and shuffled me back towards the office building. In the dark near the water, there was a little utility shed of sorts. The door was open and it led to one of the staircases.

The fact I had swam out here made me laugh. Laughing made me hurt. The pain made me cling onto Mikhaila even more.

"Come on, let's find the exit."

6

Waking

A dog was barking when I woke up in darkness. I could hear the scrabbling of paws, then the stomping of boots. Someone shouted, "We've got another one!"

Inhaling hurt. I choked on dust and tasted dirt. The longer I was awake, the more I realized that I wasn't in the dark. I wasn't blind. It just wasn't until things started moving that beams of light began to reach me. "Hello?" My chest burned and when I let the breath out, it felt like I couldn't suck more in.

"He's alive! Come on, I need more hands, more hands. We gotta get this off him!"

I squinted my eyes but all I could see were hazy streaks of orange light. Then they started lifting the rubble off of me and I could see the sky. A hazy overcast splashed by the setting sun. Bulky figures loomed over me, crawling down through the rubble with flashlights and rustling clothes. Firefighters.

"We got you. You're going to be alright. Can you stay with me? Talk to me if you can," the man said as he pulled rocks off me.

"Ribs," I said, wincing in pain as he pulled a filing cabinet off of me.

Someone else crawled into the hole with us and took my hand. They squeezed my palm with one hand and checked my pulse with the other. "Don't talk then. Can you squeeze my hand? Just like that, yes. Okay, we are going to have to move some stuff off your legs. Can you feel your legs?"

I squeezed as hard as I could and focused on wiggling my toes. It felt like they did. "Yeah," I gasped out.

I rolled my head back and stared at the sky as they cleared the concrete from the desk, then lifted it off of me and pulled my legs out. They didn't try to pull me out yet. There was a pressure on my left arm and I could feel that it was twisted wrong. I wanted to tell them it was dislocated but I couldn't get the words out.

"Just wait, you're going to be alright." There was a new person, a woman. She didn't have protective equipment on, which let her slide in near my head with a bag of supplies. She rubbed something onto my head like she was massaging my scalp. It burned bad, but not worse than my ribs. When she started bandaging me up, I got an idea what it was.

Soon enough they pulled the rubble off of me and lifted me out. I felt like I might have been able to walk, but I didn't complain as they put me onto a stretcher and rushed me down. At last I got a look at what had happened.

The building had collapsed and toppled over. There must have been an earthquake. Probably right at five minutes to four. I remembered falling right before I woke up in that place, and now I figured I had finally landed. Awoken from the nightmare and back to reality, but the memories didn't fade like a dream.

Some time after they stuck an IV in my arm, I started to wake up. There wasn't an ambulance available to take me to the hospital, so I was still laid out in the park, between those ugly statues, with a dislocated shoulder swelling up. When a nurse stopped by, I asked, "What time is it?"

"About six. We'll be able to get you to a hospital soon... I don't think they're going to be digging many more people out."

"So, it's been two hours?"

"Yeah. Don't push yourself. You have at least one broken rib, probably more. You need X-rays."

"Did you rescue anyone else from my office?"

"Plenty."

I grimaced, but didn't have the energy to specify. I laid back down in the stretcher and relaxed. My questions were only answered after I was taken to the closest hospital. They had just put my shoulder back in and I was drifting on painkillers when the curtain around my bed was pulled open. Mikhaila stood there, blinking at me.

"Hi. So, you found me," I said. Talking was easier when I couldn't feel the pain. The brace around my chest helped too.

She hesitated, looked away, gestured around the room. "Lucy is here too. She has nerve damage in her arm. Doctor's don't know why, but they think she'll recover."

"Like it was cut off and reattached?"

She nodded and closed the curtain. "I hear Ed drove himself home."

"And Seamus?"

"He was one of the identified dead."

"So… did that all really happen?" I asked.

Mikhaila shut her mouth and took a seat at the foot of my bed. She twiddled her fingers together and hung her head. "Did you ever wish you could get a do-over?"

"Yeah, I think I've wanted a do-over more than most people. But time only goes forward."

"We could pretend otherwise," she said, a smirk growing on her face.

"Hey Mikhaila," I said, and she turned to look at me with her dark eyes. "I've had a crush on you for a while. Do you want to go out with me?"

She smiled and slid a hand across the bed to grab mine. Her fingers were warm as she squeezed me. "I'd love to. You were the first guy to ask me out, did you know that?"

I squeezed her back, and it felt like I could feel the tremble of her heart through the palm of her hand. "I didn't want to miss my opportunity."

"Did you have a proposal for a date?"

"Yeah, but it's a crummy one. Just gotta do it before I forget. It's so hard to remember a dream after you wake up, you know? And they won't give me a paper to write on or anything."

"Does it have something to do with laying on the couch healing? Watching movies perhaps?"

It was my turn to smirk. "Actually, I want to go for a

hike and go looking for a certain burial spot a little girl told me about."

She arched an eyebrow at me. "When did she tell you that?"

"That's a secret. I'll let you know if we find it. And then… well hey, it's one way to get a promotion, right?"

Mikhaila laughed. "That's even more ruthless than what Lucy does."

"Maybe she'll be working for me, soon enough."

"No, she'll have to transfer somewhere else."

"Why's that?"

"Because I want you to myself," Mikhaila said, and leaned over me to kiss me.

Thank You

If you enjoyed this book, please consider leaving a review on your platform of choice. Every bit of word of mouth helps, it truly is the best way for an author to build their audience.

If you would like to see what else James has written, please visit his website, jameskrake.com

There you can find samples from his works, including his BASTION/Blackstone series, a collection of cyberpunk detective stories. Or Infinite Money Glitch, a hybrid heist adventure story set inside a video game; can some of the lowliest NPCs pull one over on the very system that rules them?